homeward bound

homeward bound

Jacob Glatstein

*Translated from the Yiddish
by Abraham Goldstein*

Thomas Yoseloff
New York • South Brunswick • London

PZ
4
G555
Hq
c.2

SBN 498 06656 8
Printed in the United States of America

HOMEWARD BOUND

II

As the liner eased from the pier, I looked for a remote secluded nook in which to struggle with the conflicting emotions deep within me.

Like exotic sea plants the red, yellow, and green lights of small craft flirted with our vessel, which was creating an ever-increasing sphere of loneliness about itself.

To flee more quickly the sentimental reminders of relatives, family, and terra firma!

The *Olympic* promptly broke loose from the earth and became a small planet with its own inhabitants, civilization, and even invisible director, whose existence might be denied if one so desired.

I lay on my bunk in the cabin and it rocked me to and fro. Sleepily I thought of Sholom Aleichem's Fishel Dovid the *melamed*, who used to ride home for the holidays.

And I too was going home, home, home to the rhythm of the rocking, until I had not the strength to keep my eyes open.

II

On the second day that famous couple, sky and water, appeared.

At first the sundeck looked like a miserly, delimited prison walk, but I gradually became accustomed to going round and round it, and even experienced the sensation of having really gone for a promenade. However, because the same faces brightened up at me after every lap, and the boat was barely rolling, and the sun was caressing us with kittenish warmth, the stroll on deck began to look like an intricate, well-rehearsed dance. Even those relaxing on the deck chairs seemed to be part of the dance troupe.

"This is a dream of a trip! The end of June or early July's the time for traveling to Europe."

My neighbor on the warm bench spoke meticulous English but enunciated the "s" as an "sh," just like a Lithuanian Jew. However, I felt certain that he was not from Lithuania. He looked like a laborer and spoke like an intellectual, selecting his words carefully, precisely. His voice was somewhat hoarse, but came from the chest rather than the throat.

He pointed out a small cloud and classified it instantaneously. He was a teacher, he confided.

"Of clouds?" I asked.

"No!" He burst into a healthy, peasant laugh. "Of physical

8

science, in a school in Schenectady."

I always loved the sound of "Schenectady." Schenectady! Like cracking a hard Turkish nut. I inquired if he had known Steinmetz.

Of course he had known the electrical wizard. What a man! What a Socialist! A quiet, straightforward, and friendly person who could talk to the most obscure individual as unassumingly as to a brother.

He uttered the word "Socialist" with a nostalgic gleam in his blue eyes. His hoarse voice quaveringly breathed forth the drily scientific word with much tenderness. He gesticulated with his massive hands and let one rest on my back as he asserted once more: Yes, sir, *he* was a Socialist!

All of a sudden he snapped out his watch and rose hastily. It had been a pleasure, and he would return directly to resume the conversation, but, begging my pardon a thousand times, right now was his time for a bowel movement.

"Heh, heh"—good-naturedly he slapped me on the back—"a man is no more than human."

He had become accustomed to a specific hour and moment. Whenever a delay occurred he had immediately to take a laxative for regularity, because that was very important. A human being is no more than a machine, he explained.

"Glance at these until I get back." He tossed a batch of pamphlets at me and stood off at a slight distance. He almost burst with laughter when he saw my bewilderment at the strange language.

"Swedish?" I asked.

"No, Danish."

I thumbed the pages, turned them back and forth until words began to nod in recognition, and I could discern the old Teutonic roots beneath their Danish disguise.

On board ship one gets to realize to a degree the worth of the individual. You begin to feel at home with the thought that though you may indeed be Moses-great, all the other passengers

9

also have something to tell. During all of that period in which you did not know them, they had lived exciting lives and they usually wished to air their experiences.

My Danish friend had been an orphan from infancy. He had not known either parent. A lonely waif, he had begun to work at a very early age, for a morsel of bread was worth its weight in gold even among kind people and next of kin.

He had so much to tell. He started with the first sharp memory, when he lost his faith—which to him had been a glowing warmth as of hundreds of melting tapers in a church—the day his village was shaken by a terrible tragedy. A fishing boat had foundered and the entire crew of eighteen drowned.

The entire village wept—mothers, fathers, brides, children, wives. The mournful bell in the center of the town tolled forth the catastrophe.

Such tragedies were not uncommon in the village. However, when they did happen, one could not help but shudder, and young children would gaze with horrified eyes at the sea laving the beach like a cold-blooded murderer.

Nevertheless, eighteen men was quite a catch for even the piratical North Sea, and all of Denmark was shocked. A very prominent priest was sent from Copenhagen to eulogize the luckless fishermen. When he learned that the dead were not members of his church, he condemned them all, in a fiery eulogy, to purgatory, forever and ever, amen!—merely because they had not had the good sense to be the straying sheep of his own fold.

The priest's eulogy caused a dreadful scandal. All the Danish newspapers seethed with it. To the womenfolk of the dead fishermen it was like salt on a wound. They yowled like cats for fear that their husbands, fathers, brothers, would fry forever in the devil's skillet.

He, the Scandinavian youth, had spat on religion and had left for America.

He became a Socialist, transferred all his religious fervor to the belief in the brotherhood of man, especially the laboring man. Karl Marx, with his dry, almost mathematical truths, became a sea

10

of fantasy for him. His heart yearned for the Utopian red sky, until the English and finally the German Socialists fouled up, and he was left simply with an interest in the cooperative movement and a hope in Franklin D. Roosevelt.

But that's quite a bit ahead of his story. At first he worked like a mule in factories. Then came the hideous war, when he became a sailor. Finally, after the war, he freed himself from the dreary shop and became a quasi-intellectual of genteel profession, though his bones still ached from the weary days and nights spent at physical labor, and there was almost no strength left to enjoy his calling.

After sweatshop work, teaching was decidedly the way to live! As a teacher in a high school, instead of a slave in a factory, he had time to read and meditate—devil take it!—upon the mystery of the universe. How had Dehmel put it? *"Nur zeit, zeit, zeit!"*

A cultured worker has better friends too. He'll never forget a dear friend, a priest now dead, a fine person, though not a Marxist—nevertheless with a deep-rooted sense of justice. A true American who respected to the letter the Constitution's affirmation that all men are created equal.

This priest had an odd weakness for globes, and owned a magnificent collection. He was a geographer and loved to spin the earth before his eyes and muse about lands and people and God's blessing on all.

Once, while visiting the priest, he noticed a new globe which, from the standpoint of handicraft, was sublime art.

"Why, this is *the* globe you've been seeking all your life! This is art of the highest kind! Who made it?"

The priest had answered with an exasperating indifference, "No one! It created itself!"

"I thought," the Scandinavian chuckled, "that the priest had gone mad. But he stubbornly maintained that the globe had created itself."

Finally the geographer had taken pity on his atheistic friend and made himself clear.

"You can't believe that this wooden globe, a mere

11

representation of the world, created itself. Yet you are ready to swear by Darwin and Karl Marx that the great, beautiful, wonderful universe with its billions of stars and planets is self-evolved."

"Wasn't that a wonderful lecture on religion?" the Dane said trustingly. "Somewhat primitive, but moving in its childish logic. That was the kind of a man he was, a man who believed until the very moment he died."

My Danish friend was past forty when he married. His wife, a quiet, grateful woman, was nearly the same age. She brightened up the evenings at home. At last twins came, a boy and girl, a wonderful blue-eyed pair. He went crazy for joy. He saw a purpose in life. But the twins lived only three days and died almost in the same breath.

"I stand there," he resumed, "gazing at the two dead little faces and meditating over my great misfortune, until the last rays of the setting sun fell on the waxen figures and I saw a great light. The infants—the boy and the girl—were really a little man and woman, my own father and mother who had left me alone in the world during my infancy. Now they had reappeared to restore my lost faith to me. The doll-like faces smiled tranquilly and I bowed my head low before the revelation. . . . I told my wife about it, but she was silent. She remained in this benumbed melancholy of silence for several months. But I suffered tranquilly, for I believed once more, with a renewal of faith.

"Another child came. This one lived, but my wife became seriously ill."

Doctors advised her to return to her native town in Denmark. She departed with the child, and this was the sixth consecutive summer that he was visiting them.

Of course it was a hard life! His wife was not well. She was kind, gentle, devoted. He could sleep with her only five or six times during the summer—the only five or six times in the year, for he was no longer the young fellow to go philandering. If only he could let go whenever the fluttery high school girls thrust their young breasts right into his face, making his head spin. He knew

12

about all the goings-on between teachers and pupils in school, but he was a self-disciplined individual—the Scandinavian in him. So he went home to his room, to the old housekeeper who prepared his meals, to his dog, radio, and books on cooperatives.

No, he did not drink—a beer occasionally—smoked four or five cigarettes a day, and when lustful thoughts came to tease and annoy him persistently, possibly if he were younger he might have decided to write to his wife clearly and to the point. She would understand and forgive him. "But Gladie, my friend, hair and teeth are gone, and something else too no longer functions as in youth. So this must be my life. The question simply is whether we're all making fools of ourselves. Is there a hereafter, or is the joke on us and on our invented righteousness and conscience?"

All night long I thought about the twins, and the reincarnation of parents who sentence themselves to nine months of pain and to a fresh death in order to bring encouragement to their orphan son—almost a chassidic anecdote in a Scandinavian setting with the saltiness of the sea and a fugue of death.

I even attempted a poem about it, but it was too much like Masefield and definitely non-Yiddish.

III

Only one and a half days on the ocean and all notions of duty—obligations to the home and the community—have already dropped from me. I breathe deeper and more freely, for I have escaped at last from the entire abracadabra of my existence as a per diem writer, as a Jew in such a bloody world that actually demands my pound of flesh.

I am at ease now, and the sunshine is so pleasant that I drive away a thought which keeps nagging at me. People pass me by as apathetically as I gaze at them. I may observe with half-drowsy eyes and listen with half-stopped ears, and am under no obligation to speak to anyone. If I wish, I may give more attention to a speck of dust than to all the passengers. I am warm and comfortable. I have disposed of my estate of poverty and have retired from everything. I am a pauper who has accumulated so much poverty that I can afford to retire from my acquired wisdom and emotions and from the hustle and bustle which is my little world.

And when faces float to the mind's surface, they seem to be submerged in a pool, with me above, tossing pebbles to make them recede and vanish.

The ocean that had been motionless until now and as if frozen—"a painted ship upon a painted ocean"—suddenly came to life as leaping porpoises appeared alongside. They emerged from

14

the water in pairs, tens, scores, of them, but always in pairs, like elegant, wonderful hands, and dove back into the waves. The sun was reflected from their backs in a magnificent display of the spectrum. It was as if a window on the ocean's surface had been raised to reveal the singular life swarming below.

The thought which I have been driving away finally overpowers me and whispers that I am lucky indeed to be traveling in the summertime without any specific mission, without even the most minimal assignment of a reporter.

My journey had brought me face to face with my boss. I had worked for collectives almost always. The morsel of bread—with or without butter—that I earned, fell from heaven like manna. I had never seen my provider, had never felt the gap between him, the absolute ruler over my livelihood, and myself the producer.

When I worked for an insurance company, which employed hundreds, I was part of a vast hierarchy of subordinates and superiors. I had never seen the bright visage of *him*, the all-powerful ruler. Once someone with an aristocratic combination of baldness and gray hair did come in. He observed us all and moved his lips as if he were counting sheep. He appeared dignified enough to be the Lord knows what, but my surprise was great when I discovered later that he was no more than one of the score of vice-presidents.

My co-workers were submissive white-collar men and outwardly well dressed girls, most of them from poor towns in New Jersey. They came to work by ferry—not so much to work as to the city of golden opportunities where, like Cinderella, one might become the possessor of the glass slipper, or at least of a fur coat from the boss for slight favors. On hot summer days the girls stank of a myriad-scented sweat, and my heart would ache with pity for the pretty faces and tripping little feet that could produce so much poison—as if they were beautiful little beasts defending themselves against male attacks with these odors.

A day came when the sun shone enticingly and I looked for a chance to rid myself of the dusty documents. The opportunity came soon in the form of a fatherly note from my supervisor reminding me of all my neglected duties. He gently emphasized that without the duties I would have no rungs by which to climb to higher and ever higher goals. I answered with an insolent memo—in that firm things were done in the grand manner, subordinates and superiors communicating with one another by memoranda. The supervisor lost no time in sending for me and demanding my resignation—actually in those words. And for the $75 a month, with the "chance for advancement" that I was getting, the demand for my resignation sounded so ministerial that I walked out with head held high, like one resigning from the Cabinet.

My colleagues, who had been my friends up to now, promptly got wind of my rebellion, buried their heads still deeper in documents so that they would not have to bid me farewell, lest—God forbid!—that might identify them with my revolt. Only one, a Scot, had the courage to say good-by. He had one word in his vocabulary—"horrshite"—which he would use both in approval and censure. With it he would dispose of the rotten eggs served us in the restaurant, and with another inflection it would pass for admiration for the pretty and friendly waitress. Only his voice would disclose whether he was thrilled or vexed. He ran after me, squeezed my hand warmly and uttered "horrshite" with so much anger and dolor that, freely translated, it meant: "Don't take it to heart, my friend, for it's all *vanitas vanitatis*, and you'll surely get another job." All this and much more that was inexpressible lay hidden in the magic word of the dear Scotsman.

It was midsummer. To reach the door I had to pass the girls' section. Their cosmetics were stewing in sweat and I was more than happy when I at last reached the street.

When I worked for a union local I never saw the "big boss" either. True, I had a manager over me. However, I felt that I was in the employ of the working class. And it was no sinecure. After the week's work the dues-paying worker, with nerves on edge and standing in line to pay his tithe to the union, would quite often vent his anger by shouting at me behind the grating that I was a leech sucking his blood and living on the marrow of his bones.

16

And at that time I was getting all of ten dollars a week!

It had ended with the manager sending me for several bottles of whiskey for a carousal of labor leaders who were giving themselves a party in self-appreciation of their work. Inasmuch as I had no money, merely instructions to a nearby saloon to charge it to the union's account, I persuaded myself on the way that, as a university student made whiskey-errand-boy, my dignity was being trampled underfoot. It was a good excuse for me not to return to union work.

As an instructor in a Yiddish school I was certainly working for a collective. In a remote town in the Catskills I had to masticate spiritual pabulum for the children as well as for the adults, most of them tubercular, who sat in their shops all day in the wintertime without doing a penny's worth of business, waiting for the summer's redemption. During the long winter nights they used to nag teacher for stories, literature, history, Judaism, culture, and what have you. On the other hand, on Sunday evenings they would appear at the meeting well-dressed, freshly shaven, and accompanied by their grotesquely fat or skinny wives. Sunday evening was theirs. They made windy speeches, argued with and insulted one another, and ferreted out bits of gossip. The women participated actively in the discussion, broke all rules of parliamentary procedure, and would try to get me to declare publicly whose side I was on. I had to be a Disraeli to extricate myself from such situations—my every smile was weighed, measured, and interpreted.

Then, in my presence the children's parents would take up a collection to meet my weekly salary. Usually it would be two or three dollars short and this would lead to a long, oppressive pause. The women would look at me with pitying eyes and sigh at my plight. But the pause would be broken heroically. A redeemer, a Lohengrin, would rise and, with earnest face and the pride of a philanthropist, put down the few dollars with a grimace indicating that never again would he perform so noble a deed. And what would they do next week? Thunder of applause. In a fistful the crumpled, greasy dollars—from the butcher, shoemaker, plumber, iceman, merchant, tailor, grocer, hotel owner, furniture dealer, bootlegger, and a childless woman married to a Gentile and inadvertently donating her mite for Jewish radical education in the belief that this would guarantee her a place in Paradise—would be handed triumphantly to the teacher.

For eight years I worked on a newspaper without seeing my boss, until the day of my journey neared and I had to go to him begging.

A busy individual, he disposed of me in a trice. I sat huddled in the chair facing him, knowing that he wished to get rid of me quickly. I too wished it were over.

Embarrasssed at finally seeing the only one, the mighty one who held the loaf of bread over me, I sat humbly and probably looked like a youngster. My straight posture, my talent, my three slender volumes of poetry, my self-confidence—everything was gone, because at the office door I could clearly hear my wife wailing and my three children pleading that I make no false step, utter no harmful word. True, the sun was shining outdoors, but there could be no talk of resigning and casting away my daily bread. Bow lower, *pater familias!*

"I'll see."

"Thank you! Good day!"

No answer. But finally I had seen my provider, seen that he considered me only a debit, an ink mark in his ledgers.

Coming out chagrined, with glowing left ear and flushed cheek, I met my foreman. His first glance was one of sympathy. He himself knew too well the taste of such visits, but he quickly straightened up, so that in my helplessness I might not consider him a comrade.

The bit of joy over my first journey in twenty years had cost me plenty, and a strange twilight fear had enveloped me.

Because of great fear I had fled directly to the vessel.

IV

In the morning when the ship's news informed us that Hitler—taking at face value Mussolini's counsel that one dare not rule with the same individuals who helped engineer a revolution—had butchered his close friends, I began to search for Jewish eyes and ears.

The miniature newspaper, attractive in layout, presented the news about Hitler elegantly, calmly, and without comment, as though it were no more than a "thrill" for the hundreds of passengers. After the rich a la carte breakfast they were serving the heads of a dozen of Hitler's pederasts on a silver platter—part of the fine program aboard ship to ward off boredom.

The Gentile passengers got no thrill from the news, however. They thumbed the pages, read the jokes, the sports items, the afternoon's entertainment program, but scarcely paused over Hitler's blood purge.

When I tried to elicit some comment from them, their responses were phlegmatic. Many admitted that they had not seen the news.

I felt lonesome and sought a "warm Jewish heart" that might help me laugh, cry, but in the Jewish accent.

First, the Jew in slippers. A respectable looking Jew with a trimmed beard. He was sitting on a bench, poring over a Hebrew volume. His lips mouthed the sacred words, but one did not hear his voice. A handsome, neat, well-dressed, aristocratic Jew.

Beautiful, delicate hands that turned each page with contemplative reluctance as though sorry to go on while the preceding page still was so full of immeasurable wisdom. He had picked the most remote nook, obviously wishing even his silent mumblings not to reach the ears of a hostile world.

He appeared to be about seventy, on the border of the years of grace, and a tranquility that may not be purchased even with an emperor's fortune emanated from him. That "the day is short and the task great" did not concern him. He was studying for the pleasure and enjoyment of profound thought.

It was refreshing to see a Jew with the temperament of Lao Tze's aphorismic wisdon—a sharp contrast to the average American Jew who has accepted the truism of actuarial tables that one drops dead at fifty-odd.

He radiated the Sabbath restfulness that hovered in our home like a secret, when father and mother had shut the door and were taking a nap after the *cholent* or Sabbath roast—a tranquility that would remain undisturbed until my father took down the bolts and iron bars from the store front. The smell of iron rust, the frozen clanking of keys, and the first customer of the new week would be the signs that the God of Abraham had lit all the lamps and that the holy Sabbath had ended and the week with its worries had begun. . . .

Suddenly the Jew's slippers linked up my first seventeen or eighteen years at home with my present journey to see my mother. "Her ears are yellow as wax," my aunt had written. "Pack immediately and come, and may His Blessed Name avail that you still find her!"

So the ship was now traveling back to my youthful years as though it were floating back in time. The two decades in America have suddenly crumbled to dust in my hands. Most important now are the early years which, like two hollowed-out parts of a toy, strive to become joined, to attach themselves to all that is destined for me at home.

A flood of autobiographical fragments rush in on me from all sides. I struggle against the temptation to submit my early years to the scalpel now instead of some twenty years hence. However, I yield slightly and begin to reconstruct my past as I have never done in all my twenty years away from home.

My Lublin—that possessed no sights except a town clock and a firewarden who, until midnight, while everything slept (except the stirring legends around the synagogue), sounded the quarter, half, and full hour on a trumpet—is not even recorded on the small maps; only on larger ones can one locate a thin line of barely visible characters: Lublin.

Long before the embryo: a paternal great-great-grandfather Enzel and a grandfather Yossel Enzels. (I had known neither of them; to me Enzel was no more than a word sounding like a surname.) The family archives, that is the older uncles and aunts, had the former inscribed as a Jew who had earned his water for soup as a sexton—a quiet Jew who had never uttered a harsh word and who by all his actions had aroused the suspicion that he might be one of the Thirty-Six Secret Saintly Ones. My grandfather Yossel Enzels, however, was more like flesh and blood, a kind-hearted exploiter in whose workshop were sewn the gowns for children of the nobility, the governor's daughters, and very wealthy women. He employed about thirty girls, who ate and slept on broad tables in his shop. There they trilled their love songs, accumulated their dowries, and were married off.

My grandfather was no great scholar, but he piously observed the exhortations of the "Israelite's Laws," and participated in daily group prayer. While the house would be surrounded by phaetons waiting for Yossel Enzels personally to fit the wedding clothes, he would be praying devoutly, knowing that they would wait. Connoisseurs claimed that he was actually a botcher of a tailor, but he had personal charm and a way with people.

Yossel Enzels died of grief because my father, his sixth son, went into the Czar's army.

On my mother's side: Polish village rabbis and a great-grandmother Dresl who had been left a young widow. When her husband died, Grandmother Dresl had already been six weeks with child. Since this might have led to ugly gossip, she forestalled the chatter of foul mouths and announced at the cemetery, before

21

the burial, that she was pregnant and that, God forbid, no one should spread false rumors about her—so wary had she been of what people might say! And if that wasn't enough, she made doubly sure by naming her daughter Binya after Benjamin, her husband.

Because her husband had been a pious soul, my great-grandmother obtained an important community concession—assistant at the bath-house. I knew my great-grandmother and remember her very well for the meticulous way she fulfilled her duties. It seems that my mother still looked upon me as little of a male when she took me along to the women's bath. I would be set down on a wet bench, while the younger and elder women splashed about in the water in accordance with all the rules, as good Jewesses should, under the strict and competent supervision of my great-grandmother.

Her son, poor thing, was left an orphan at seventy, when his mother died at one hundred. Grandfather Avrom was a widower, who lived with us as far back as I can remember. He was a pillar of the household, just like my father, mother, and brothers.

Grandfather Avrom had a beautiful white beard that had become slightly tarnished from the use of snuff. He owned many snuffboxes but they were all proletarian of bone or wood; not a silver box, let alone gold.

Grandfather's ablutions took much longer than a prima donna's. Before making his appearance on the street he would polish his boots, comb his beard, and inspect himself in the mirror. At the door at last, he would call me over for the final inspection, lest, God forbid, a feather still clung to him. Every Friday he would go to the bath-house and still have time for a nap after his return before leaving for the chassidic rabbi's house of study to welcome the Sabbath. And at our home it was the custom that no one touched the Sabbath loaf until grandfather had recited the benediction.

He was a goldsmith and owned strange tools. The queerest of all, for melting gold, was a bellows that would fill the house with dense smoke. He used to clean rings, earrings, and brooches gratis

22

for the entire family except my mother, who would have to quarrel with him for a good number of weeks before he touched her jewelry.

Sometimes he would go off with his pack of tools to the small towns and return with a fine deficit, which he would have to cover with several good-sized drinks of brandy and a tasty meal. After such refreshment, grandfather would turn as red as a beet and his blue, carefree, childish eyes would grow heavy-lidded. Soon he would be stretched out on the bed and snoring into his lower lip and beard, which would rise and fall rhythmically.

We children in the house would have to walk about on tiptoe because mother, half in mockery, half in command, would warn that grandpa, the great breadwinner, had just returned from far-off places and was grabbing a snooze.

The ship was barely rocking. The Jew had dozed off. The air had become sharper, and from the ocean came a wondrous cool tang of water that had been warmed for a long time by the sun.

The second Jew was not so easily recognizable. He was walking arm in arm with a diplomat from Haiti, who spoke a beautiful French, to which the Jew listened attentively. He was in seventh heaven whenever he could inject a sentence of his own in French.

The diplomat, much taller than his companion, bent forward constantly so that his own height would not be accentuated too strongly.

When I abruptly accosted the shorter individual with the news about Hitler, he stopped in his tracks like a hypnotized cock. For a moment he did not stir, then involuntarily released the diplomat's arm. The slender mulatto, as though nothing had happened, took the arm of a lady and continued his stroll with her, while his erstwhile companion gazed after him with a look of childlike bereavement.

What made me take him for a Jew, he asked, as if he had met with some great misfortune, for after all he is no Polish Jew, but from the Netherlands!

He had a cross-eye that kept disappearing and then coming out

23

of hiding. The conversation was a sort of duel, and he waited for me to take the offensive.

"I'm definitely a Polish Jew," I threw out challengingly.

He favored me with the gentile's compliment that I didn't look it. When I asked about his ancestry, he refused to reveal himself even through his great-grandfather. What nonsense about Spanish Jews, immigrant Polish Jews, Baruch Spinoza! He was descended from a long line of Dutch Jews—and there!

I tried to steer him into philology, and asked whether he heard the old fashioned Dutch-Yiddish still being spoken in his family or perchance somewhere in the Jewish ghetto of Amsterdam. He merely supplied the scanty information that he was descended from wealthy merchants, had made a short three-week visit to America, and was now returning to his father's business.

The Jews in Holland? He was reluctant to speak about them at all, but finally expounded that they were primarily good, patriotic Dutch citizens, with a strong interest in politics.

"By what are they bound to the community of Israel?" I inquired.

"By nothing!" he emphasized sharply, pleased at this opportunity to isolate the Dutch Jew. The Dutch Jews are a singular phenomenon. A kind of thirteenth tribe without history and traditions. Undiscovered apocryphal documents may some day throw light upon their origin. (He was an intelligent person, but obviously preferred to bandy naivetes rather than come out with shocking truths.)

Slowly however, he did talk. It is embarrassing when the Polish Jews in their ridiculous garb and long, matted beards, go shuffling along the Amsterdam streets. The Dutch Jews try to segregate themselves from these folk, but it is somewhat difficult to convince the gentiles, and some degree of criticism falls on the Dutch Jews too.

"Why have they come to disturb the well-established tranquility of our great-great-grandfathers? I blush when I see a Polish Jew. Why must they attract attention with their stubborn non-conformity?"

24

"Why should that annoy you?" I feigned stupidity. "Does a Chinese bother you? A Hindu? A Negro? I'm beginning to suspect," I baited him, "that you aren't the emancipated Dutchman you pretend to be, since you must bear on your shoulders, like a yellow patch, the shame for the Polish Jew who is neither your uncle nor even your nephew."

He let my barb pass without comment and explained how iron-strong the Jews in Holland had felt their position to be, until *that Hitler* began to stir up things.

"However, for the present there's no anti-Semitism evident. All are equal. We have Jewish ministers, judges, magnates, and everything would be peaceful, but with Hitler not far off. . . . The Dutch really have no great love for the Germans, but who can tell?"

"So you're afraid of Hitler?"

He admitted that he did not feel quite secure.

"And this Hitler-fear involuntarily makes you a brother of the other twelve tribes of Israel?"

I grew tired of this parrying. My young 200% Dutchman probably thought that he was speaking with his own voice, but I heard the well-known raucous voices of my brethren in their vari-climed and multilingual adaptability.

"Nevertheless, separatist-Dutch as you may be," I smiled gruesomely, "according to the very latest science, you're a non-Aryan. The race doctrine will lay its paw on you, and reach you no matter how Dutch you be. And, my dear friend, a full seventeen million Jews, not merely some 600,000 German ones, are now non-Aryans. You and I, the Polish-American Jew, when we look at ourselves in the Teutonic mirror, are equally non-Aryan."

I wished to leave, but now he would not let me. He desired to talk about Jews and Judaism, as a person sometimes wishes to scratch a wound. So I again reduced the discussion to simple questions and posed this foolish one:

"When you hear that Chinese are being massacred in China, and Jews in Germany, what concerns you more?"

"As a civilized being I wish both to affect me equally, or to be equally of no concern. Nevertheless, I must admit that the news about Jews hits nearer home."

"Why?"

"Why?"

We had asked the question simultaneously.

"Perhaps," he explained, "it's personal fear that suffering of Jews in general will ultimately reach the Dutch Jews. And that would be an injustice, because Dutch Jews are so different. As I explained before, they're Dutchmen first and Jews afterwards."

He became chatty, and showed off his bit of culture, mentioning philosophers, authors, musicians, while I thought of a kitchen picture—a Dutch mill, heavy wooden sabots with upturned toes, foolish flaxen hair, and engrossed fingers milking a cow; and of Kanitfarshtan, the hero of my primer years, the hero who lived and laughed and died all in one day. . . .

"Recently," he droned on, "the Dutch Jews began to suffer from zionism, which took hold of our youth like an epidemic. A cousin, a highly cultured young man from a wealthy family gave up everything and went off to Eretz Israel. Why should such a chap who had wanted to become an apostate suddenly become a Zionist? Actually the most estranged Jews became active in Zionism. This is Hitler-panic probably," he consoled me, but himself even more. "The good Dutch Jews look askance at such Zionistic flirtations. It's harmful. It might even destroy the respect of our neighbors, a respect which the Jews cultivated so assiduously and with such care for generations. Zionism is a great danger to us! If the Dutch were to discover that our hearts lie outside the boundaries of Holland—"

"Why don't you become an apostate?" I asked suddenly.

He was not in the least insulted. His imbalanced eyes showed for the first time a glimmer of yearning. He confided that he was strongly drawn to the romanticism of the church. He consulted his father many times, but the old fellow, though unable to present any good logical reasons, had dissuaded him. One of these days he will take it up with him again. Unless he were to go off to

26

Palestine to see for himself. Perhaps he would hear there the diapason of the Jewish voice calling together the children of the *diaspora.*

Diaspora . . . diapason . . .

How more beautifully and more sincerely he would have expressed it with Jeremiah's: "A voice was heard in Ramah, lamentation and bitter weeping; Rachel weeping for her children."

At the end he dissuaded me from visiting Holland, should such a thought ever occur to me. "There's nothing to see," he said, calling forth his little swivel-eye as a witness.

However I suspected that he did not wish still another Polish Jew to sneak into his Holland. Who can tell how much harm one Polish Jew might do!

Unnoticed by me, a tall, broad-shouldered fellow had been eavesdropping on my conversation.

He informed me that he was from Colombia, from its capital city Bogota.

"When I tell you Colombia, Bogota, with the accent on the 'a,' do you have any idea where I live? You just hear names. If you know geography, well and good. In any case, you don't really know it.

"And if I tell you that I live in South America, do you think that'll be any easier for you? South America and *South America* aren't alike. You're traveling from New York, so I'll try to give you a little description of where I live. Imagine that you've gone mad, God save us, and you're set on going to Bogota. You get on a ship in New York and sail for seven days until you come to a small town, Carthagena, in Colombia. But whoa, no farewells yet! You're not there yet! Your troubles are just beginning!

"You take a train to the Magdalena River. The Magdalena is the true *Sambatyon,* and the little red-bearded Jews who live on the other bank are we 'apes,' the peddlers who hustle and bustle to keep the pot boiling.

"So we're at the Magdalena. You travel by boat. Boat! A wreck, a wooden affair that drags along—one day, two, three, four, five! Then all of a sudden you're on a train. What happened? The Magdalena is indisposed. Right there it's her whim to have a waterfall, which is good for neither boat nor passengers. So you must go around it on a train until you come to the Magdalena again and continue on your way. Then you come to a small town and take a train again, but this time to Bogota, with the accent on the 'a.'

"The train goes up and up until you're four thousand feet above sea level and riding by coffee forests. You see beautiful plantations and coffee drying in the sun.

"The coffee trees like the cold mountain air. A sapling no taller than a man loves to have you slave and slave over it. It's like the building of Pithom and Ramses before you get a little coffee into the house. A coffee tree must be nursed and coddled before it produces.

"The coffee berries look like red cherries. They're picked by hand, and the soft meaty part of the berry is thrown away. Only the hard kernel which is the coffee bean is kept.

"Well, so you got a free lecture too, and just because you're riding to Bogota. Serves you right! You ride along like that for hours and hours, passing many pretty villages, until you come to Bogota.

"Now be obstinate and say that I don't live on the opposite bank of the *Sambatyon*! Here's my cheek and smack me one, but a resounding slap! Don't worry, I can stand a wallop and I certainly deserve it too, because I've buried my best years there.

"Perhaps you think I lost at the game? I've made a fortune, but it isn't worth a pinch of snuff to me. My mother's yearning for me and my homesickness for Bessarabia are worth much more than the $80,000 or let's say the round sum of $100,000 that I made. . . . What is man anyhow? Is he just a pig, a hoarder of money? Or must a man, in addition to having money, feel that he plays some part in life too?"

The tall Bessarabian narrated how, in 1922, when he was twenty, he went to Ecuador, from there to Peru, and in the very first year made $10,000 by peddling.

Why Ecuador? How does a Jew happen to go to Peru? Don't ask questions of life. A friend got him to go to those places. To

28

this friend he owes thanks for the good fortune that sticks in his throat like a bone.

There were a thousand young men already peddling in Peru. He had always been a promoter, an organizer, and immediately became their manager. He loaned them money and merchandise and made his thirty per cent profit.

In 1925 the atmosphere in Peru suddenly changed for Jews. The peddlers had to run off and of course forgot to pay their debts. He went bankrupt.

Chile is also a country. So he popped up in Chile, dealt in hides, and soon had $25,000. As can be seen, the Supreme One is a Father, and a hard-working young man doesn't get lost. With his capital he came to Bogota, Colombia, in 1929. Thus began the chapter "Colombia"—may it sink into the abyss!

In Colombia he found several wealthy "Russian" coffee magnates and a few hundred Jewish young men—*boys*, they are called there.

"Why boys? Very simple—because they aren't married. That's where all the trouble is. You see, four hundred young Jews go around, peddle, make a nice living. If one of them wants to set up a home—as the Bible teacher—to lead a respectable family life, there's no one to do it with.

"Go deeply into our situation—a whole country without Jewish brides. No *shadchan*, no *badchan*; neither marriage broker nor bard can help. The wedding canopy stands unused. It's a terrible pity. Everything is with the buttered side down, because there's no Jewish wife with tender hands to grab a fellow by his mop of hair and say: 'Time you amounted to something!' Without a wife, life is just hustle and bustle, no roots, nothing! Jewish houses stand empty and lament. Around the houses are trees, and they lament too. Life is as normal as a pea sticking to the wall, and just because there's no Sarah, no Rebecca, no Rachel, Leah, Deborah, Braindle, Zlota. Not one to be had! So you walk around like half a person—one half is in Bogota and the other half, the mate, doesn't exist.

"Bogota has about thirty well-established Jewish families that

29

haven't been long in the country and haven't had time yet to raise marriageable daughters. The few that there were we caught up on their own terms, and now we're waiting for the young ones to grow up—like waiting for the Messiah. What can you do? There are none!

"So you go around hungering and wifeless. Some of the boys went off on the adventure of intermarriage with the Spanish-Indian-Negro girls, but they've been no great success and are very poor examples for the other boys.

"Why don't we import some Jewish girls? Let them be ugly as death, cross-eyed and slightly pockmarked, for us they'd still be beautiful. Their luck would shine like the sun! We'd fight over them! We'd sing serenades to them under their windows! But what woman is crazy enough to come to Bogota?"

"But how is Jewish life in general?"

The Bessarabian took his time. Calmly, deliberately, but with a flow of words that apparently had been lying deep, deep within him, he sought to arouse my sympathy for this marooned tribe of his, tried to throw upon my shoulders responsibility for these newly acquired relatives in their out-of-the way community.

And my shoulders bent lower and lower under the heavy weight of Jewish brotherhood, Jewish blood—the burden of a whole world of Jews! Not only in Rumania, Poland, America, Russia, Holland, France—but also Hindu Jews in Calcutta, yellow-skinned Jews with almond-shaped eyes in China, Yemenites, even Falashas, Arabian Jews in Algeria, Spanish Jews in Greece; and if that wasn't enough, the Bessarabian now added Jewish suffering in Colombia.

"The Jews aren't liked much. We're known there as the 'Russians,' and they hate the Russians. The Colombians like the Germans—rave about German technology and machinery. When the Hitler episode began the Germans among us started their propaganda, and it took well too. We were afraid to do anything about it—to take a German to court. The Jew knows in advance what sort of justice he would get and who would win.

"Maybe the climate is good for the natives; but not for Jews.

30

Cold, rain, dreary weather. You go around with a sour face all the time. There is little rain in Peru, but in Colombia it pours, and when it does it drenches body and being.

"What holds the young men together? Loneliness.

"We have a kind of society—*Ezrah*, mutual aid in case of need—for those who have to be set on their feet again. Yom Kippur also brings us together somewhat. But it's not because of the Jewishness—it's because of the fear. We remember the prayers *Kol Nidre* and *Unsahne Tokef*, so we hire a room and gabble some liturgy. But the whole year long we're without religion, observe neither Sabbath nor holiday, and we work like mules.

"Do you think we have a *shochet*? Not even for the several dozen Jewish families. Little by little we learn to eat *trefeh* meat, may it bring us no harm. A while ago we bought some land for a Jewish cemetery. That too we learned from bitter experience. A few young men turned up their toes and had to be buried in the Christian cemetery. So we worked until we bought a strip of cemetery land for ourselves.

"So death is taken care of, but life is bitter. Don't think that I yearn so much for the *shochet* or the prayers. If not a prayerbook, let there at least be a Yiddish book, a newspaper. But to have nothing at all—you simply become a lousy yokel. If you're not religious, at least know something. But we're just plain ignoramuses.

"So we're back where we started—healthy young men without wives, unable to establish a home. Nevertheless they don't do any fasting. Every one of them has a mistress.

"The dark Colombians are pretty, devil take 'em! Slender, tall, graceful. You imagine you'd be the happiest person in the world with one of them, but they're not worth a damn. As cold as an iceberg. Lies there like a duchess and doesn't show a sign of life. But they're the only women you get, so you must adjust.

"We know that Yukel lives with this one, Shmuel with that one, and Chaim with another. She keeps house for you, and you live with her like a wife, but don't openly reveal it to the public.

"Are they faithful? The devil knows! It appears they are, but

31

it's hardly reasonable to suppose that they have no earnings on the side. Because no sooner do they have some sort of complaint than a Colombian male pops up. Where did he come from? Fall from heaven?

"You can live with her this way for a few years until you become fed up and try out another one. But they're expensive delicacies. They aren't fools.

"For instance, for two or three years I lived with a mulatto and she cost me five or six thousand American dollars. Suddenly I 'turned cold to her'—that's the way she put it. When she began to call me to account, as if she were a wife, I dropped her.

"Then I first realized—I'm ashamed to say it—that I was in love with her—what's more, so accustomed to her that I couldn't live without her. I'll confess to you as if you were my brother, that when I returned to her I went on my knees to beg her forgiveness. She cried and said that I broke her heart, and then she showed me the door."

He took a snapshot from his breast pocket—a mulatto beauty, tall, full-bosomed, of lusty carriage, proud.

"You see her? I had to leave my business in strange hands and travel around the world in order to forget the whole thing."

He sighed, hitched at his trousers, and loudly blew into a handkerchief. For the moment he had forgotten the Jewish troubles of his Bogota.

Suddenly he realized that he had been meandering too long about himself. He recalled that he had just been the chronicler of the small Jewish community in Bogota, and resumed his role of historian, bearing the entire responsibility for four hundred *boys*.

"That's the way the boys live. They have no wives, so they have love affairs. When you leave your mistress you must be a 'gentleman,' do it quietly, and leave a nice gift of money too. Otherwise she might hire someone to put you out of the way. And if she isn't lazy, she can do it herself—they can handle the dagger, the Colombian women!

"But what else can we do? A man can't sleep, night after night, all alone in a bachelor's bed. You can't hang a lock on human

32

nature. You can't show the thumb to the Evil One, who doesn't let himself be swindled or driven off with incantations.

"We're so hungry for wives that some among us pick out a little Colombian girl who's still going to school. The young man immediately negotiates the marriage and brings her up. For the poor Colombian parents it's a stroke of luck. The Jew pays her expenses and rears a wife.

"We have several couples like that. The Colombian women have even become converts, and so far things are going along smoothly: the young women are accustomed to their husbands from childhood on. One of them, a delicate child, fainted twice last Yom Kippur but she completed the fast. And even though they're so much younger than their husbands, they stick to them, their 'governesses' who raised them, almost on their knees to be little wives. But such fortunate cases are exceptional. How many people have the patience to pick a small girl and sit and wait?

"In short, you see for yourself that it's far from a pleasant life. When Sunday comes you go around all morning collecting the debts of the week. In the afternoon you sit down to a game of cards, at which a great deal of passion is spent as well as two or three hundred dollars. Then you take a bath to wash off the dust that collects during the week, and you sit down again to play cards. At night you go to a dance hall where you hire a girl for six cents a dance.

"If you don't have a mistress you take home some poor Colombian woman who comes next day to collect her pay in goods. On Monday you get up with a bitter taste in the mouth and go back to working like a mule.

"Passover is somewhat of a break. Some forty young men get together in a house and stuff themselves and get drunk. The *Hagadah* isn't read, but the gluttony is a souvenir of the holiday. There you have all of our spiritual life. It's lucky that the Jewish cemetery is flourishing and waiting for the end!

"But we're different from that Dutch nincompoop! We're ignorant Jews, but with a spark of Jewishness! He's a Jewish freak! If we got a ninny like him into our hands!"

33

The banging on the copper tray announced supper. It had become somewhat cooler on deck, but the Bessarabian hadn't yet reached the end of his story.

"I must get away from there," he exclaimed. "What can a Jew like me do in New York with capital? Let's say I came to visit for six months. I'll find a girl, marry her, and then remain in the country. But I can't sit down and write *mezuzas* for doorposts! What can I do with capital in New York?"

"You can publish a Yiddish newspaper, a good Jewish weekly." I blurted out the fantastic bit of advice from sheer embarrassment at being entrusted with a fortune of $100,000.

"I? A Yiddish newspaper? How come? After all, no evil eye, I'm a first-rate boor."

I comforted the naive Bessarabian: it did not really matter. Culture and the publication of a Jewish journal do not necessarily go hand in hand. One need not be educated. It's a business like any other.

The word business he understood very well.

V

Except for a lemon-green-complexioned old maid who puffed nervously at a cigarette as she circled the deck, and several other chronic recluses who greet one with a loud and crisp "Good morning" or "Good evening," clearly indicating: We give no more and expect no more!—friendships were already springing up and cliques forming. Individuals were extending their antennae and seeking each other out. Everyone found someone more or less his equal.

Just as there are some passengers who shrink and recede into themselves, so there are others, good mixers, who have a natural aptitude for mingling with everybody. My Danish friend was such a hail-fellow-well-met. In one day he knew everybody and everyone knew him. He knew the life story of everyone on board; and promptly made everyone's comedies and tragedies common knowledge. He was even a matchmaker of sorts, bringing together unhappy members of both sexes. He loved to have things popping and merry.

He came over and declared that he had a rare find for me, a Russian, a real Russian. He felt that a Russian and a Jew are in-laws after a fashion.

And Chazhev the Russian was delighted with me too. Apparently the Dane and his camaraderie were too much for him, even though the Danish-American teacher spoke about socialism

35

and the great Russian experiment. The Dane was also satisfied, for he had many obligations and many acquaintances, and could not stay too long with any one.

Chazhev evidently felt at ease with me. His small, friendly, almost Mongolian eyes gazed at me trustingly.

I never was in the old nor in the new Russia. I knew Russians only from my Polish-Russified town with its Greek Orthodox bearded priests, its Russian *gymnasium* or secondary school instructors, and its military officers. One glance at Chazhev was enough to reveal that this was a new type of Russian before me, and not because he had become sophisticated or Americanized as a result of his three years at Cornell University, where he specialized in electrical engineering.

He was delighted to be going home, and was particularly gratified at having been able to complete his "four-year plan" in only three years and thus save the Soviet a full year's expenses.

The expenses were not small! The Soviet government paid his tuition and gave him $150 a month to live on. For a student this meant lordly living. The Soviet also supported his wife and two children while he was away in America. Now his country was awaiting him. He was proud to be returning home not only with a diploma but with knowledge which he would be able to apply to the daily life of reconstruction in the Soviet. He thrilled at the prospect of demonstrating that no money was wasted on him.

He saw all of America—Ford's factories, General Electric, and other models of big business. He had warm words for America, but for no money in the world would he settle there, because. . . .

He was very careful in his choice of words, was as tactful as a diplomat. He was grateful to America for the education he got. He was leaving—why then speak ill of the country? He considered himself an ambassador sent by the Soviet to a friendly power—why then, by some tactless remark, involve his country in an embarrassing situation?

He would like to be home already.

"You see," he told me, "my elder son was born mute. When I left home he was five years old and couldn't speak a word. He would just sit mute and look kindly at everybody. He took after an uncle who was a tender-hearted mute with an innate sense of beauty. The uncle never uttered the wild shrieks of other mutes; he spoke only with his fingers and in his own way was laconic. The son too used to sit as silent as a giraffe. During recent years however, eminent Soviet professors took the child in hand and, for the present, have succeeded in teaching him a solitary word, 'Papa.'

"Now, when I get home, I'll hear it with my own ears! I can hardly wait! You can't imagine what a joy it'll be to hear the silent Mischa say 'Papa.' He has been saying it all the time with his eyes—you should have seen the agony—with his lips, with his hands, and now he will actually say it with his voice!"

Tears ran down his cheeks as he talked.

This was not a mere father's love, but a native son's devotion to his country, whose gifted professors could achieve so much progress and perform miracles in the fields of medicine and surgery.

Chazhev's father was a peasant but had always been a revolutionary, though scarcely knowing how to read and write. He knew full well the meaning of "laborer," "peasant," and of the czar's knout. He had been imprisoned several times and, thanks to that, was now half-paralyzed and a human wreck at sixty. He gets a government pension and weeps for joy at having lived to see such times. "You should have seen his pleasure when I was attending the university and used to sit studying all day long. Sometimes, after taking a drink, he would grab up a thick physics or chemistry text and order: 'Come on, Vasia, read some of this! Let's see how a peasant's son reads and gets smart.' I had to please him and read whole passages, and when he, the peasant still affected somewhat by religion, heard the strange soporific words, his eyes would fill with tears and he would exclaim in a choked voice: 'Slave tye gospodi! Slave tye gospodi! Praised be the Lord!'

His mother can neither read nor write. She was always a hard worker, with coarsened red hands, swollen feet, and red-rimmed puffy eyes from grieving while his father was in jail, the children ill, and little more than some stale bread in the house.

Such are his antecedents. And now his country has opened all gates and doors to him, the peasant's son! Where would he be now under the Czar? The very lowest, commonest, filthiest dirt underfoot. But in the Soviet Union he, Chazhev, was a select student. His country sent him abroad, confident that he would acquire enough knowledge to be of help in the development of the land which must set an example for the world and be a model of a new way of life for future generations.

Why shouldn't his heart overflow with gratitude? But not for selfish reasons alone. A new life was rising—at present a hard life for many, many millions. But one could already discern signs of a better future. He began to enumerate the benefits of Soviet rule. He was very cautious, shrewdly choosing only those qualities that plainly revealed the shortcomings of the United States, which he could not criticize openly.

"And not only should we peasant sons be thankful," he said, "but the Jews ought to dance in the streets, yes, dance in the streets! What were the Jews before the revolution? Nothing! And now what are they? Everything! Just as every citizen in the country is everything!"

He was not speaking in the manner of a Christian professing a love for Jews. There was no trace of that about him. He stated it simply, very happy that his USSR had corrected a great wrong, a grave injustice. He was thoroughly familiar with all Judeo-Soviet matters. He knew about Jewish schools, collectives, writers, and was enthusiastic about the Jewish "little theater." He paused over these matters not as one would over curios, as a non-Jew might sometimes drop into a synagogue to listen to Hebrew melodies; he catalogued them as great achievements of his country.

He was thirty-four years old, of medium height, and truly peasant-like in appearance, though face, hands, and eyes had taken on some refinement. He had shrewd eyes clouded by a mist of genuine Russian sorrow—warm eyes.

Warmth! That's the word. He glowed with warmth. He spoke with the kindliness often found only in individuals who are healthy and well-rounded personalities. He talked and talked, describing his country, which he had traversed in its entirety; and while doing so he injected regretful remarks about still unremedied faults.

Only once, in passing, did he mention 'the chief.' The comment was not accompanied by any force or pretentious praise. He was interested, sincerely interested in the *whole*, the *grand*, the *vast*. "It's unfortunate," he said with almost a peasant naivete, "that other countries don't realize it and don't as yet emulate us."

Following this bit of propaganda, he informed me that there was a sizable Soviet group on the ship. He indicated a corner of the deck where a woman was seated on a deck-chair. Her legs were stretched out—not delicate, aristocratic ones, but unquestionably feminine legs not too badly shaped, considering how far the Creator may toy with proportion while imparting some grace to heavy limbs. At her feet sat a number of young men.

She was the only one on board suffering from seasickness. Her jet-black hair, parted in the center, her Jewish eyes, her full, seemingly swollen lips showed it.

The young men looked up at her, and competed with one another in phrasing tender thoughts, chivalrous expressions, and well-turned phrases. They called to aid verses from Lermontov, Pushkin, Nekrasov, Mayakovski and Yesenin, and the Russian-Jewish lady was pleased by this royal attention. She kept complaining of her seasickness, and her cavaliers were at her service. Prettier women than she were left companionless, but for the Russian youths there was a world of charm in the Russian words from feminine lips, on an English ship, in strange surroundings. surroundings.

"Children, take your dreamy eyes from the elegant Sonya Yakovlyevna and spare a word for a gentleman too," Chazhev said in a sprightly and affected tone. "Let me introduce you!"

A straw-blond chap with a deep Chaliapin-like baritone, another with the face of a simpleton but remarkably merry and gentle eyes, a third wearing a beret and with very restless hands, and a fourth with the somewhat stooped back of a student—all leaped up as at a military command. Sonya Yakovlyevna extended a small hand that had readily adapted itself in the metamorphosis from housewife to coquette. In less than a minute I was one of the group.

"Puzhalusta," the blond youth boomed in his wonderful baritone. His free gestures, ready speech, and ringing resonances awakened in me an echo of Bazarov, and a breath of Sanin with his sex emancipation, and scores of other imaginary heroes whose manners were imitated by an entire generation of Russian intelligentsia. The blond fellow was exceptionally well posted on politico-economic matters. His friends evidently respected him for his dialectics.

He and two others of the group had been sent to the United States for a six-week inspection of plants and factories. The fourth youth, with the doltish face, had won a factory lottery for a trip around the world and a year's vacation. So he had seen the world and was now returning to the factory.

Sonya had spent ten years in America. Two years ago her husband had left for the Soviet Union, where he obtained a responsible position. Now she was to settle there, and was going joyfully, for she had retained all her Russian qualities while in America—her name, her father's name, and also her Odessa-hard though quite mellow Russian with its Yiddish *r*'s.

I invited them into my cabin for a drink, explaining that I had several flasks which I could not tackle by myself. They fell silent and looked at the straw-blond youth with the lank, stringy hair. They, Soviet folk, were somewhat ill at ease at finding themselves being coaxed to drink by a stranger.

The blond fellow laughed in embarrassment. His eyes began to glisten and he half-shut them as he thought of the liquor. He appeared Pan-like while fencing with the idea. After a silent compromise between the "tempter" and Soviet dialectic, he decided in the affirmative.

"Nyemnozhetchko!" and he indicated with his finger that he would take just a drop.

All followed me, even the indisposed Sonya Yakovlyevna. And

40

after the blond fellow had poured down a good number of *nyemnozhetchkos*, my cabin resounded with gay Soviet songs.

While they sang and danced, while curious and sober heads kept popping in to stare at our merrymaking as upon an orgy of amiable cannibals, I said to myself: This is it. Not questioningly, nor as an exclamation, but with drunken indifference. This is it, I said to myself. This is the new, joyful, healthy generation of materialistic romanticism. This is the result of victory, of captured barricades, of struggle, of revolutions and communes. This is a song of achievement.

That I too was sitting there with the victors was no opportunist's hop, skip, and jump onto the bandwagon. I lived through all the revolutions in history, with all the names of revolutionary martyrs, with all the working-class slogans tattooed on my childhood brain by my birthplace, which had fought, suffered, and helped to overthrow "dear old Nicholas."

> Brothers and sisters, march on together;
> A plague take Nicholas and his mother!
> Hey, hey, down with the police;
> Down with the autocrat of Russia!

I used to tease my grandfather with this Russian revolutionary doggerel which class-conscious dressmakers, seamstresses, embroiderers, carpenters, turners, tanners, wire-drawers, and butchers' helpers would hum stealthily under their breath. It was my childish rebellion against his fear.

"Just listen to him spout!" my grandfather would exclaim angrily. "We'll all be sent to Siberia because of this rascal!"

I would continued unperturbedly and would also get my brother, two years younger than myself and barely able to say "aristocrat," to join me.

I was only five or six years old at the time. My playmates were snot-nosed urchins with shirttails sticking out, and narrow-visored Jewish caps. I remember that the ground still did not feel secure

41

underfoot, and we all toddled about while playing "czar." We must have looked like a yardful of penguins.

I do not, God forbid, wish to embroider myself with revolutionary glory, but even then I already knew that the palace, or the jail that was visible from a great portion of the city, was not reserved only for thieves. Armed ferocious soldiers patrolled it day and night. We could see the jail from the entire palace evirons and from the various Jews' streets as far as the synagogue. Jews went to *shul* under the fear of the government, for the soldiers' guns were always staring down at them from the hill above.

At the foot of the jail stood Krasutski's factory in which work-worn, stoop-shouldered, coughing cigar and cigarette makers slaved. Between factory and jail, particularly that section housing the political prisoners, there was a bridge—the kindly daughter of the Krasutskis. She was lame, wore spectacles, and had a Gentile-Jewish face and serious eyes. At dawn she would go out on the balcony and fearlessly converse with the prisoner-heads in the little barred windows.

My grasp of rebellion? My grandfather used to tell me revolutionary tales about Berek Yoselovitch and Jewish tavernkeepers who would conceal priests, and about these very priests who after crawling out from behind the oven would twirl their mustaches and shout at the Jew: "Off with your hat!"

My grandfather—he was a hardened realist—related that whenever the Cossacks caught a revolutionary, they would sever his most important member and hand it to him with exaggerated courtesy: *"Kuritye pozhalusta,* have a smoke please!" He also had reams of stories about resolute, stubborn guerrilla battles in dense Polish woods, and about gallows, lances, daggers, and Cossack knouts. . . .

First steps of the revolution. Past midnight. Singing is suddenly heard, not in the ostentatious main street, but on the humped and terrified Jews' streets. The half-cardboard huts, glued together with early-morning spittle, tremble awake, but remain neutral and mute.

42

We know what it means. We are even afraid to look out of a window; we curl up beneath the featherbeds. We know that revolutionaries are taking a street by force, risking it in the expectation that the deed will be accomplished before the arrival of troops. From the tyrannous Hesse's foundry where heavy scales are manufactured, from the brickyard and from the sugar refineries, the Polish Socialist party groups come marching with torches and banner, singing:

> Atop the barricades, workers,
> Raise the red flag!

At first they march slowly, then quicken their pace. The torches flash by the windows, and all at once, quiet—frightening silence that cries "Help!" Suddenly there is heard a galloping of fiery-spirited Cossack ponies which, as expected, have come too late and after all is over.

The Cossacks are aroused at having arrived late, and appease their anger with a rifle shot, which is riveted into the Jewish night like a red-hot nail. . . .

Once, on the eve of Tisha b'av (the Ninth of Ab) the night of lamentation for the Destruction of the Temple, the "comrades" got the desire to demonstrate revolutionary courage and to march through the synagogue yard with their banner. Soon the Cossacks came galloping up with knouts lashing out. The synagogue was hurriedly locked from within. For several hours the Cossacks could be heard snuffing about its walls like enraged dogs. Nevertheless they did not dare enter. We, on the other hand, were afraid to leave, and after the Lamentations, remained in the synagogue that entire night.

What a Ninth of Ab! We all actually experienced the Destruction! The candles flickered out. The cantor remained seated on the steps leading to the ark. I sat and half-dozed on a hard, overturned lectern, shuffled my stockinged feet in the straw and enjoyed the fleas that trickled my heels with their frenzied

43

attempts to reach the flesh.

In the center of the synagogue the large, awesome silhouette of a chandelier swung to and fro like a dangling corpse. In my ears still reverberated themes from the sorrowfully dramatic verses "Mourn for Zion and Her Cities," which the cantor had just been chanting with the entire congregation.

I was dreadfully hungry and thought of the famine before the Destruction of the Temple, when parents had eaten their children. . . . We are being besieged. . . . Titus' murderers are running about outside and I will soon be devoured here! Fearfully I looked at my father, who was fondling me with a sleepy hand as he half-dozed. . . .

I do not remember exactly which pogrom it was, whether the one at Kishenev or at Byalistok or some other blood bath. That day my father came home with the paper and wept so bitterly that everyone in the house cried with him. My mother, my brother, and even the mute servant blubbered—all except me, whose heart would turn to stone when it came to crying. I gazed at the black-bordered pictures and at the caption "Martyrs," and thought simultaneously of the Ten Martyrs and how iron combs had torn the flesh from their bodies. A dead *shamus* with a scroll of the Torah in his arms. Dead children with staring eyes. Torn books. With uncertain thoughts I had already vaguely grasped at that age, the significance of Jewish rebellion—on one side Nikolai and pogroms against Jews, and on the other, young men in blue, black, and red shirts with tasseled belts. They, the shirts, wished to drive Nikolai from the throne.

I could clearly visualize a Pharaoh-like Nikolai, his every word a command or a decree against Jews, seated on a high throne. Like Xerxes he holds a golden scepter and wand, and bathes in Jewish blood. As he is about to issue a new and stern decree, red Yankel Stoller and pockmarked Yossel Shlisser suddenly burst in. They accord him the proper respect, rattle off the "His Imperial Highness," and having rendered Nikolai his due, say to him unceremoniously, "Lord Sovereign, get the hell out of here!

44

You've ruled long enough!" And when they kick him down from the throne, they fire several bullets into him, spit three times, and shout, "Take that for the Jewish blood you spilled!" They grab a pole, press a spring, and out flutters the red banner. And they march forth with song through all of Russia:

> Hey, hey, down with the police!
> Down with the autocrat of Russia!

Nevertheless my heart ached whenever the "shirts" occasionally took over the *shul* and, as my teacher the *melamed* phrased it, stood up to slander the Lord. Against Nikolai, I could understand; but against the Jewish God! How was the Jewish God to blame, the God who is abused, whose scrolls of the Torah are trampled underfoot, whose Jews are slain—the God who is in exile together with Israel his people, and who does not have a single happy moment except perhaps on Simchas Torah, the Festival Day of the Law? What could one have against such a God?

This Jewish God of mine looked just like the rabbi of Lublin, Avramele Eiger, a skinny, quiet-voiced Jew with long white beard, white stockings, and slippers—an individual who did not know what money looked like, who took no fees, who fasted on Mondays and Thursdays, and got along on nothing every day of the year. With quavering voice he was always lamenting Jewish tribulations. Such was the appearance of my persecuted, childish, Jewish God. What could one have against such a God, who wished for the millennium each hour of the day, but whose hands were too frail and too weak to bring the Messiah?

It was on a Purim, the festival celebrating the defeat of Haman, that the "shirts" seized the Maram synagogue, locked the door, and the leader, with long black hair, knelt on the rostrum and began to speak: "Comrades and citizens, today is Purim. Today, they'd have you believe, a miracle happened. Today, they tell you, God rescued the Jews from a pogrom—"

"Down from the pulpit, you scoundrel, you traitor in Israel! May a thunderbolt lay you low! Down from the pulpit! May your bones rot!" resounded the voice of Moishele Glisker, a *cohen* of the priestly lineage, with a fiery temper and a brow that always lit up like a cock's comb. "Down from the pulpit!"

The threats of the "shirts" that they would leave him a cold corpse, that they would put a bullet into him, did not help. They went up very close to him and even displayed a pistol, but he continued shouting as if at a fire, "Down from the pulpit!"

I cannot be blamed for having been on Moishele's side in this struggle between the speaker against God and Moishele Glisker against the entire revolution—and revolution meant against Nikolai for the Jewish blood that had been shed. He was my hero, the Mattathias with the ready sword and the battle cry, "Who is unto God—come with me!" I stood near him like a little Maccabean and *we* fought the battle of God, who could not and would not fight himself because he is compassionate, a weakling, a softling, a whimperer, a weeping shadow swathed all day long in prayer shawl.

To this day I cannot stand defiance against God. No matter how often I recite the dictum, "Religion is the opiate of the masses," it does not help. Whenever anyone begins to insult the helpless Goodness behind the whole mystery of misery which is called life, I feel myself deeply insulted at this mixing of groats and beet-tops. I know that this will not even begin to disturb my children, for they knew neither Avramele Eiger nor the quiet, gentle Lublin rabbi, Reb Hillel Lifschitz. They never heard his broken-voiced sermons before the blowing of the ram's horn on Yom Kippur, nor the anguish in my uncle 'Chiel-Asher's cadenza-like flourishes on the shofar.

Nevertheless I felt that a new power had appeared in town. Until then the strong-arm fellows of the underworld, the chaps who were nothing loath to plunge a knife between one's ribs—Avramel Rutzer, Mordchele Benkert with the lacquered stiletto, and other such fine specimens—had ruled by force. Anything they said, they meant. If they threatened, it would be carried out. If they happened to be beating a prostitute brutally

46

and she screamed, "Jews, children of mercy, help me!" the children of mercy would pass by as if they had not heard, for it's a pretty face you got if you started something with the likes of these fellows.

But when the "shirts" made their appearance, the underworld lay low. I once saw the Bundists belabor a thief who had taken several rubles from a poor servant girl. "Hand over the money!" They kept whacking him until the blood gushed, and he had to return the money to a groschen. Not until the servant girl, with hands as red as frozen apples, said "That's enough!" did they quit.

It was a new power, which also attacked, but differently. It was for an ideal. However, I became somewhat confused when the new power entered the shop of Elya Taub, who had stubbornly refused to give his apprentices a raise, and put several bullets into him.

Man and child wept at his funeral. Elya Taub, a tailor, had been far from rich. When I saw the black casket on the Jews' street, his crime against the workers seemed trivial compared with the punishment. His wife tore her hair, his children wept, and the lads from the Hebrew school were singing the psalm "Righteousness Precede Him." I weighed the two on a child's scale yet they somehow did not balance.

Elya Taub's death cast a dread over the entire town. For the first time one began to feel that if it were really so, that "all of Israel are brethren," with common interests when it came to praying to God for a favorable judgment or merely salvation and consolation for Jews, nevertheless, all year round there existed two factions: workers and employers. It was the first class-conflict shooting in town.

The workers sang their songs more happily and more proudly. Whenever a cluster of eight or nine of them formed, a tenth would immediately appear and begin his propagandizing with "Comrades and citizens!" Elderly Jews, when passing such groups, would mutter skeptically: *"Az es vet nisht vern besser, vet vern erger.* Times'll either get better or worse."

I was not at all surprised therefore when Simeon Berger was brought to our home. My father worked in Simeon Berger's shop.

47

The yellow-bearded Reb Simeon had a large clothing store and a fine dwelling on the main street. My father used to visit him on holidays to pay his respects, but for Reb Simeon to come down on an ordinary Wednesday to our house behind the palace—only the new "power" could achieve that!

Several strange young men with stern, earnest, and business-like faces sat at the wide table beneath the kerosene lamp. Simeon Berger, seated definitely not at its head, was wiping the sweat from his brow. My father actually was at the head because he held the onerous position of referee. The new "power" had faith in my father's honesty and justness, although he was not completely class-conscious.

Simeon had smacked a youth, an errand boy, and had been summoned to a hearing. The young messenger had a piping voice like a choir boy's. He kept leaping at Reb Simeon.

Simeon Berger would wipe the sweat from his brow and try to answer, but my father would commandingly cut him short.

"Perhaps you'll keep quiet, Reb Simeon? You've probably forgotten about Elya Taub."

This was enough to silence Reb Simeon for several minutes, until the errand boy, much like a rooster, would leap at his face, and my father would again have to invoke the ghost of Elya Taub.

On the table, as warrant of peaceful class struggle, lay a glistening new revolver. Little flames from the lamp flickered on the bluish steel.

My father rendered the decision. Reb Simeon Berger was to pay an allotted sum to the "party" as compensation. The errand boy was to get a raise of half a ruble a week and cloth for a suit. Reb Simeon was to promise to keep his hands to himself and to refrain from striking anyone, because—the young errand boy finished for him—"nowadays y'can't go around smacking people!"

Reb Simeon accepted the decision. The "party" was satisfied, and when it had gone, Reb Simeon, with raging eyes, was left seated opposite my father. He rose and began to pound his head with his fists.

"Itzchok," he shrieked at my father, "I'll kill myself! I'll hang myself! If I can't hit my own worker any more, why live? If I can't have the pleasure of soundly smacking such a snot-nose across both cheeks and showing him who's older, what am I here for? What am I living this filthy life for?"

Yes, long before Nikolai did Simeon Berger feel the revolution, and yield. Never again did he raise his head. He went about hunched up and gloomy. In him the revolution celebrated its first victory.

Then came unsettled times. The party commenced with a bad doorkeeper—no watchman, but the true Cerberus of the court—and all because he went to extremes in serving the czar. He looked disdainfully at his broom and mop—for him these were mere incidentals when compared to his nobler duties. He was most meticulous about informing and keeping an eye on suspicious tenants. His children went about in rags and begged the Jewish children for bits of *pletzl* or onion roll. His wife used to get drunk and wallow on the floor and curse her husband and children with the vilest of oaths, but the watchman himself was a sober individual. He was convinced that the "scoundrels" were likely to stage a revolution under his very nose and he fulfilled his duties with a chancellor's punctiliousness. One dawn the career of this, the czar's most faithful servant in town, was brought to an end.

After this beginning, constables, patrolmen, and even an assistant to the mayor were shot down. Once, on the Jews' street, I remember hearing several sharp reports, as if someone were hastily rapping a stick against a shutter. A patrolman who had just purchased a bag of flour fell several paces from me. The contents of the bag powdered his whole face, but streaks of clotted blood began to break through the chalky mask, looking like blobs of liver and lung. The dead patrolman, in his polished boots, lay there for a long time; and until the "law" from the other side of the town clock came, held an inquest, and took him away, the Jews felt as if he had been planted for a blood libel.

The Abele Tzimring affair occurred about the same time. No Jew in town had a beard longer than Abele's. It was veritably an ornament for the face. With hands clasped on his behind, he

49

would walk slowly as if strolling, his large dark eyes peering from beneath bushy, black eyebrows. He was already as gray as a dove, except for his eyebrows. He would cast a glance here and there and from time to time remove his right hand from his backside and slowly stroke and fondle his gray beard. His glance was a form of inspection, and the first lad encountered would be called over.

"My boy, no one ever lost money by looking. Have you prayed already? Here's a *groschen* and buy yourself some ice cream."

No one ever took the groschen, because Abele's kindness gave one an immediate cramp.

Abele was a Jew who had entry to the town hall, the city bureaus, and the county seat. He was on the closest terms with the department heads. It was no secret that Abele was an informer and that he had acquired several apartment houses by that means. In his youth he had made a living from the recruiting office only, but in later years had begun to inform on political offenders too. In town they damned him but trembled before him. His glance was feared, but he, in complete unconcern, and dressed in his long satin greatcoat, would go snuffing and spying along the Jews' street.

Bullets seemed to have no immediate effect on him. Once he was shot and slightly wounded. Several days passed and he was at his business again. Another time he was shot and wounded seriously, but the happy tidings came from the Jewish hospital that his condition was improving and that he would soon recover. Government officials transferred Abele to the Russian military hospital for safety. The army hospital, surrounded by high, thick walls, was under heavy guard at all times, but a few young men managed to sneak in to "visit the invalid" and did him in on his sickbed.

Abele's funeral was a cheerful one. No instruction took place in any *cheder*. Although Abele, while alive, had been somewhat of an official and had been feared, we all felt that as a Jewish corpse he was entirely one of *us*. The coffin bobbed along hurriedly on the way to the cemetery, and woman and child along the road threw stones at it. Abele Tzimring with the broad beard was buried

50

somewhere near the fence, and for weeks Jews openly took pleasure in the job and even justified it with the Biblical quotation, "You shall remove the evil from your midst."

At that time the czar decided that he had to show the town his cursed power in order to throw such a fear into us that we would no longer have any desire to challenge his authority. A patrolman more or less, yet the power still rests with him!

First marched the drummers—*boom-tarararoom, boom-tarararoom.* They led the parade, which was really a demonstration of military strength. The drummers were there to call together the town to see the artillery, infantry, grenadiers, and Cossack cavalry. The Cossack horses were so wild as to be uncontrollable; they kept breaking from the ranks and whirling around and around in circles. It was a wonder how a Cossack with his rifle, lance, sword, and knout could keep from falling and breaking his neck. Other riders on tamer horses led the artillery. The cannons, with their exposed muzzles, dragged, rattled, and jolted along the unpaved streets. The stern and cruel faces of the troops were turned toward the gloomy houses that lay enveloped in fear. Ahead of each company marched drummers who kept beating out their *boom-tarararoom, boom-tarararoom.*

The townspeople, however, not only did not come running, but shut door and gate. Instinctively they felt that this was no mere parade. The drumming cast them into a dreadful despair. As matters stood, the nights were already long and frightful because of martial law, and here they were coming to poison the days as well! All the shops were closed—business was shot to hell anyway. Jews ran; Jewish women, like hens, called their broods together. One gate after another slammed shut, and the entire Jews' street appeared deserted.

I alone did not manage to run through the *cheder* gate quickly enough. The gate was a high one and I must have looked like a small frightened kitten trembling throughout the long military parade. I was perhaps the only civilian out on the Jews' street. Officers winked at me; Cossacks stuck out their tongues in order the better to scare me; even smarter fellows aimed their guns at

51

me; and when the drummers passed by they beat out the *boom-tarararoom* still more loudly as though especially in my honor, while I stood stricken by fear.

Not until the last soldier had passed did the gates begin to open silently, stealthily, tentatively. My teacher Yankel Peiletz greeted me as one long lost and tickled my face with his good beard. I was surrounded by the children who begged me to tell them everything. Even the assistant listened as I fabricated wild exaggerations. I did not omit to tell how they had wanted to capture and make a Cossack of me, but I had driven them all off with the *Shema Yisroel*—Hear, O Israel!

How I had envied the cobblers' and tailors' boys, the young fourteen- or fifteen-year-old apprentices who had to lug the water tubs during apprenticeship, but spruced up in their colored shirts after work, nibbled pumpkin seeds, and flirted with the girls. They belonged to the Assistants Bund. If someone had to be beaten up, it was their task. If a glass tumbler was to be hurled into a display window of a shop whose proprietor did not observe the prescribed hours, they did it. More than once I told my father of my envy for these guttersnipes, but he would retort bluntly and sharply that the revolution would be carried out without me. My mother too would add that they were quite capable of getting along without my help, and my grandfather would *buy* me off with a three-groschen piece to recite a chapter of the Bible. He was no great scholar, so he took pleasure in hearing me rattle off a chapter of the Bible and also throw in a bit of Rashi, the commentary. My grandfather maintained that there was no better charm against revolution than a chapter of the Bible, and "let others worry about revolution!"

At that time I had already learned of the treasure at my Uncle Velvel's. He owned hundreds of books, from Schomer to the proletarian literature of the day. He had one idiosyncrasy—he would sooner give you a *gulden* than lend you a book. He asserted that whenever he loaned out a book he missed something in the house, as if a chair or a table had been removed. To come to his

52

home and sit and read—that with the greatest of pleasure! But to take a book out of the house was strictly forbidden.

Uncle Velvel was my proletarian uncle in contrast to Uncle 'Chiel-Asher who was my teacher at that time. Uncle 'Chiel-Asher, the eldest of seven brothers, was a tall good-looking Jew, the handsomest at the baths. In his beard the black hairs still fought with the gray. His eyes were youthful. The only blemish on his body was in the corner of the right loin—a slightly bulging bit of intestine that sought to push its way out and which Uncle 'Chiel-Asher kept in check with a band.

Uncle 'Chiel-Asher's *cheder* was the third class, where one also studied a bit of Talmud or Gemorah, as well as some scriptural Hebrew.

My uncle was good-natured. He had fine little jests for every sad occasion. The children actually crawled all over him and he did not mind. His second wife, who could not acquit herself of the obligation to treat the daughter by his first marriage as a stepdaughter, nor her twins as a devoted mother should, would henpeck him, and he did not mind that either. His twins too would have pestered him, but both little girls still crept about on all fours. They crawled along and turned in the same direction, and never were separated by more than a hair's breadth. They slithered over the ground like snakes and ate off the floor. Because of the stepmother, the *cheder* children felt no love for these infants and would stealthily step on a little hand or foot, and experience a fierce joy at the stepmother's shriek, "Oy, curses on 'Chiel-Asher, they've killed the twins!"

My proletarian uncle was an operator on shoe uppers. He had discolored nails and acid-eaten hands. He thrummed away on queer, tall, wide-bellied Singer machines and sang Goldfaden tunes at the same time. He was a pauper and had a reputation for being one of the enlightened, almost a heretic, although his entire heresy consisted merely of speaking during synagogue services.

It stank of leather in my uncle's workshop. Uppers lay scattered everywhere and the smell alone made my palate dry. He had no apprentices. All alone, he stood hunched like a camel over the tall

53

machines and sang. He was the first of the brothers to turn his children into artisans. One daughter became a seamstress, one son a painter, and he even married off one daughter to a cobbler.

Bela Pearl the seamstress was a Zionist, and she undertook to convert me to the cause. I must have been seven or eight years old at the time, she probably a girl of seventeen with long thick braids. She spoke to me about Dr. Herzl and about the struggle of workers for a better life, and arranged for me to go on some Sabbath afternoon to the "party exchange" beyond the new road. However, my younger brother betrayed me, and my pants and boots were taken from me in advance and hidden away. My father insisted that even the Zionist revolution be accomplished without me, and it is quite likely that the concealed little boots put an end to my political career forever.

However, my Uncle Velvel's books were free. I devoured the Socialist pamphlets, that were somewhat too hard and dry, like stale kichel. I read heretical works, but derived more pleasure from storybooks and from Sholom Aleichem.

Because of these books I used to drop in at Uncle Velvel's for Sabbath refreshments. My Aunt Bina, who was doubly related to us—she was Uncle Velvel's wife, my father's sister-in-law, and also my maternal grandfather's sister—was a small pious woman, a kind soul who did not demand of God more than her assured mite of poverty. She would have ready for me a saucer with gooseberries, currants, shelled pea pods, and broad beans. My uncle would be lying on his back and snoring. It was a rhythmic snore, and like a cricket's chirping, would cast a drowsiness over the entire household. My Aunt Bina, who was always mumbling some prayer, would be reading the Bible in vernacular in a drowsy sing-song. She knew that the books were not quite kosher and would try to convince me that a bit of *gemorah* was much healthier for my good little head. But after such chiding she would seat herself at the window and read, with pauses between syllables, from the Bible in vernacular, while I would tremble with the heroes of "Family Tzvi." I would live through the horror of a pogrom while chewing mealy broad beans, sour currants, reddish gooseberries

54

with tiny hairs, and fleshy sour cherries that filled my mouth with the sweet-sour juice of ripe fruit. I would read Edelstadt's poetry, read a few verses, and repeatedly turn back to his picture. I loved to look at his handsome beard and aristocratic face. His "working class" appeared to me somewhat like a folk of princes who, like water carriers, suffer and bear the heaviest burden. I barely associated Edelstadt's working class with our own downtrodden workers of the town.

Once as I sat hunched over Edelstadt's poems, several shots rang out. People came rushing up from everywhere—yells, cries! I ran down the dark stairs of my Uncle's house. A bleeding person, his cap pulled over his face, half-reclined on the ground floor. The steps were bloody. In one minute the whole town knew that young Atlasowitch had been shot to death.

On the following day hectographed proclamations were plastered all over town stating that Atlasowitch, who had gone over from one party to another, had been shot for betraying party secrets.

Mothers had been wont to bless themselves with Atlasowitch. He was a pious young man with black curly hair, a white skin, and deep, almost girlish eyes. He was a good student of the Talmud and came of fine family. Atlasowitch's father was a stern, reticent Jew, but secretly his heart rejoiced in his only son. He knew that he had a genius growing up, but kept silent—to avoid an evil eye. He felt that some day the Diaspora would be brightened by his son's light.

Suddenly young Atlasowitch strayed from the straight path and his father became gray overnight. Nevertheless, he remained silent, repressed, his lips sealed.

The old man could hardly be persuaded to go to the funeral. He walked proudly, with head high and not at all like a mourner; while his wife beat her head with her fists. His eyes were like glass. Strangers were weeping and found something meritorious to say about the young sapling that had fallen a victim of the times, but the father walked on proudly and calmly.

When all the rites had been performed and it was time for the *kaddish*, and all were waiting with bowed heads, old Atlasowitch stood even more erectly, spat into the grave several times, and exclaimed loudly each time in Hebrew: "Erased be his name and memory!"

He left the several score of mourners and unfalteringly strode homeward.

After all this preparation and travail, the revolution came like a great holiday. It came suddenly. I awoke in the morning and sensed immediately that this was no ordinary day but a blessed one—just as a child on opening its eyes, even before the first thought, feels a sweet sensation in all its limbs, and the somnolent brain breaks into a smile at the realization that there would be no *cheder* on a holy day. That holiday too was sensed immediately, from the very first moment that the sun burst through the window so brightly.

On all faces, in all streets, sunshine and joy! Officers exchanged kisses with Jewish maidens. Nobles embraced Jews. Street parades with the red banner displayed freely. Song. Music. My father raised me high above everyone's head and carried me through the dense crowd.

"Yankele, don't forget that you lived to see all this with your own eyes!"

I, a skinny and pale lad, felt as if on air, light as a fluttering flag in my father's hands. The czar granted a constitution! Soldiers were fraternizing with the populace. Cossacks were laughing. Kalmucks with Mongol faces showed their white teeth. The sidewalks sang. It was tramp, tramp, tramp, all day long. Red ribbands in braids, red flags waving, people crying for joy, kneeling in the street to cross themselves. Young chassidim of the pietist sect, with goatees and billowing kaftans, leapt and sang as on Simhas Torah. My small heart almost burst for joy. Delicate, perfumed hands tickled me with flowers and tossed confetti at me. Red flags fluttered above many shops; trade was at a standstill. My father raised me still higher; I felt unsteady and insecure in his hands. At any moment he might drop me and I would be

56

trampled by so much joy, by the ladies' little high-heeled shoes, and by the Cossack ponies that stood quiet now, neighing placidly amid the populace on the sidewalks. My eyes devoured everything. The *klop-tararap* of the parades intoxicated me.

Hundreds of comrades were gathered about the jail. They were conversing with the political prisoners through the small windows. The wrinkled and creased faces wept and laughed. In a moment the gates were to be thrown open. They sang, shouted, embraced, laughed loudly in uncontrollable happiness. Ladies whom one never saw behind the palace, near the jail, were now singing together with the grimy foundry workers:

> Atop the barricades, workers,
> Raise the red flag!

"Yankele, don't forget this!"

But several hoary pious Jews glided about like ghosts, separated from all the tumult, and warned us. These kill-joys had gloomy faces and crooked backs, as though they had borne on them the horrors of 1648, of all Jewish "Destructions." They, the Jeremiahs, wandered through the crowds and warned, "Jews, go home! It's not your celebration!"

And on the morrow we spoke with shame, heartache, and fear about the horrible night, the long night of terror—the bullets that hailed on workers near the jail . . . infuriated Cossacks . . . blood . . . dogs of officers and soldiers . . . spies, and hundreds of arrests—and about Nikolai's signing of the constitution with his right hand and nullifying it with his left. Yesterday's joy still rolled on the streets, but now it had become panic. The janitors swept up the dirty confetti. . . .

The revolution was suppressed and almost entirely driven from my childish consciousness. We all grew up with merely tattered shreds of reminiscences. Overt resistance was dead. The workers' courage collapsed entirely. They had had hold of a good thing, and who knew how long it would take to achieve it again! Now elderly girls sang of nonexistent imaginary fiances instead of revolution. Crooked backs sat hunched over the machines, bowed heads sang theater tunes—

> Oh, don't be so proud of your money,
> For it can go in a jiffy. . . .

to console themselves, these "weavers of gold." Poor Sabbath summons of bridegrooms and still poorer weddings were held. Spinsters somehow or other got themselves married to anyone. Poverty increased. Scrofulous children with bulging eyes and broad little behinds splashed about in the mud puddles. From time to time typhoid fever paid us a visit. Several sensitive youths who absorbed too much of Schopenhauer and took the pessimistic hypocrite literally, committed suicide. Funerals increased. The revolution had been swept away.

And we, the select youth of the town, the fine idlers, consoled ourselves in the Saxony garden, on a dark lane, with Gorki's *Mother*. We saw the shadows of downtrodden laborers, dark factory walls; heard the call to strike; saw the fists, the strong muscles, and the image of a worker's mother, a proletarian Joan of Arc.

However, it had become an esthetic-tinged revolution. We criticized the heroes, analyzed their actions, and wondered "whether they were psychologically true to life." We appraised them in the light of Nora's slammed door—should she have left her husband or not? We read *Hunger, The Weavers*, and while the environs of the Saxony garden teemed with noblemen and commission agents and Jews who were pecking like hens at small crumbs of a livelihood, we walked about like Hamlets, twirling our canes. A twirl thus—"to be"; a twirl in reverse—"not to be."

So one of us became a bookkeeper in a sugar refinery, another an assistant to a writer of petitions to the government. One went off to the Academy of Art in Krakow, another to the Warsaw Conservatory. A third became a Hebrew teacher, a fourth secretly wondered what he was to do with a diploma without a gold medal and how his father would take the news if he were to become a

58

Lutheran. One sent poems to *Niva* and exhibited kind letters from the good Vladimir Galaktyonovitch.

And I began threatening suicide if my father did not get me a steamship ticket to America.

Sonya Yakovlyevna was stretched out on the sofa, resting her feet on a chair. The blond Russian was smoothing her disheveled hair and fondling her cheeks. She evidently derived great pleasure from his gentle hands. With trembling fingers he began to stroke her feet, as though desiring to massage away their fatigue. He affected a sleepy voice and sang Lermontov's lullaby, "Bayu-bayushki-bayu," adding after each stanza in recitative the one famous one-line poem: "Cover your pale feet!"

The steward, who had been invited to the party to add proletarian color, was drinking alone from a bottle. Feeling that he dare not be too democratic and hail-fellow-well-met with drunken passengers—for one may regret it when they sober up—he was safeguarding his reputation.

As for myself, I kept repeating the words: "This is it!"—which, if they had any meaning in the beginning, were now completely boozy. Like a drunkard who takes hold of a sentence and makes it the refrain for his entire mood, I kept repeating: "This is it!" True, my head was beginning to clear; nevertheless, to me it seemed that my Lublin of 1905 had bred and painfully reared these fine youths. My tailors, shoemakers, and seamstresses, long since in their graves, had blistered with hunger and raised these liberated young people.

Only when I was quite sober did I recall that I demanded that the Octobrist drink a toast to my Lublin; that I cursed and reviled myself in as good a Russian as I could muster; that I shouted that Moscow need not be so proud—it might condescend to recognize that there was a Lublin on this earth to which it owed a debt; that my town ought to get the Order of Lenin.

Hey, hey, down with the police!
Down with the autocrat of Russia!

And at night we sat half-sober, fraternizing in the bar. We drank Scotch and soda at a large round table and felt the vessel barely heaving. We forgot the sea, however. Everything seemed to be saturated with liquor. Our conversation acquired an even more lilting cadence, as if we were not conversing but almost waltzing.

The strains of an operatic pot-pourri—a bit of Wagner, a taste of Puccini, a snatch of Verdi, to the crescendo of Leon Cavallo's clownish lament—were audible from the ballroom.

At our table, in addition to the Russian colony and of course Sonya Yakovlyevna, were several ladies who were drawn to our circle by their urge for the exotic.

One of them belonged, after a fashion—a Lithuanian Jewess. She appeared to be at the threshold of thirty. Her face had not as yet entirely sloughed its contours of girlhood. She spoke six or seven languages, among them a rather good Russian with a German accent. She was going to visit her family in Riga, though she had been in America only three years. Her husband was a rich importer with a house in Flatbush, and she could permit herself the luxury of nostalgia so soon.

She spent the entire day with a mulatto diplomate from Haiti. Arm in arm, they carried on a flirtation in French. In her style of dress and bearing one could recognize good breeding. She had one annoying fault. Whenever she became somewhat merry and friendly, she wove an "as my husband says" into her conversation, precisely as if to emphasize that she still was a faithful and loyal wife, and not a subject for gossip.

Her delicate fingers toyed with the little glass of Scotch. With black eyes glittering, she kept exclaiming: "Well, *tovarishch*, not so bad to be alive!"

An Englishwoman well over forty was also at our table, and exclaimed in amazement:

"Aren't these Russians just exquisite!"

The blond fellow, who in his gallantry not only was thoroughly Russian but humanitarian as well, fearing lest the Englishwoman be neglected by cold-hearted men, singled her out for his attentions. He paid her warm Russian compliments. He was young enough to be her grown-up son, yet bombarded her with expressions of his love. She flushed from the imbibed Scotch, glowed with his compliments, and kept reassuring me that "these Russians are just exquisite."

Another guest at the table was a Finnish-American woman who was extremely pleased with me because I asked her what Kalevala was doing, mentioned the brothers Vainamoinen and Ilmarinen and also their bitter enemy Leminkainen. But I impressed her very, very much when, as a would-be musician, I sang for her at the top of my voice fragments from Sibelius' *Swan of Tuonela*.

She was a nurse and exceptionally grateful that I associated her with "roots," whereas for most Americans Finland was no more than a screeching sound, a word without nuances and derivation. Out of gratitude she invited me in all sincerity to her home in Hoboken.

We also had at our table a young American woman of thirty-two or thirty-three from Wisconsin. She was a head taller than tall. A teacher of French in a women's college, she had much of the spinster about her. Every now and then she slipped on a pince-nez dangling from a silver chain about her neck.

She broke up the monotony and repression of the teaching year each summer by a trip to Paris, where she absorbed ten weeks of Bohemia—and for an American schoolmistress Bohemia meant much more than the word denotes. She became a totally different person in Paris; the Wisconsin schoolmistress disappeared. She consumed the ten weeks as if they were a day. The hardest thing, she explained, was to avoid her grown-up students who also sneaked off to Paris for a whiff of freedom—so she had to resort to shady hotels on side streets.

Here on board ship she already felt herself on the eve of that Parisian metamorphosis. When she removed her pince-nez one saw a shrewd, intelligent face and a prudent restraint close to the bursting point.

She had many close friends in Paris, but they were entirely different Russians, she confided to me—White Guards. She was pleased with this opportunity to acquaint herself with the other

61

side of the Russian coin.

"The side which you know is the worn side of the Russian coin," I told her, and Chazhev remarked even more bluntly in connection with her Russian friends in Paris:

"They ought to be shot!"

"Why?" She became aroused. "They're very fine chaps!"

In order to screen a sudden little flame in her eyes, she slipped on the schoolmarmish pince-nez once more.

"You too are fine dear people. All Russians are fine," she said. suddenly assuming the role of conciliator between the old and the new Russia. But Chazhev with his limited English insisted:

"Your friends ought to be shot!"

She laughed in great embarrassment. All those jolly Parisian summers that give her the strength to endure the winters somewhere in a small Wisconsin town—shot dead!

"But why?" she pleaded in a motherly vice, as if interceding for her own flesh and blood. *"Pozhalusta,* please," she begged conquettishly while mispronouncing the Russian word. Tears welled up in her eyes and she finished with a memorized *"Ya vass lyublu, spasibo!* I love you, thank you!"

Her entire Russian lexicon exhausted, she remained seated, full of admiration. However, it irritated her that no peace could be made between her White Guards and the Bolsheviks at our table.

The couples sitting along the walls and in the corners were conversing quietly. It was already past midnight, the hour of laconic wisdom, when eyes, hands, and feet do the talking. But even the mute conversations were being carried on in the bar of the English ship with an Anglo-Saxon reserve.

Someone at our table remarked that these separate and strange couples seemed like one collective love. The laborer who had won a world tour started whistling Schubert's "Serenade."

"Comrades," the blond one shouted, "you can stand me against a wall and shoot me like a dog for being sentimental, but his whistling has struck my mood. Ordinarily the song with the nightingales has the flavor of marinated herring, but tonight I'm ready to kneel before one of our ladies and sing Schubert's song to her. Long live the Soviet power and eternal life of love!"

He joined in the whistling and cuddled close to the Englishwoman.

In the midst of this lyric outburst one of the Soviet group moved closer to me, and confided what could be readily guessed—that he was a Jew.

May the international gods forgive me, but in that colorful setting his words were redolent of dear old Jewish hominess, of freshly baked Sabbath bread, of hot, peppered fish cooling on a platter near the window, of savory chicken soup with floating globules of fat, and even freshly ground horseradish that stings the nostrils. And all this at his first statement that his father was a *melamed*, a teacher of Hebrew in a small village somewhere in Poland.

His father is a Jew, a pauper dying of starvation, and he sends him money every month in order to keep him alive. He is lucky to have got out of Poland in time, to have completed his studies for engineer and to have a responsible position in a factory. Why, the factory sent him to America for six weeks! Too bad only for six weeks! Had he spent at least several months there, he would have learned some of the language and would be speaking English by now, and not like Chazhev, who only stammers.

This last he said aloud so that Chazhev and the rest of the group might hear the good-natured jibe.

He continued to tell me how he, a Polish-Jewish *cheder* lad, had escaped from the noisome ghetto into the wide world. Had he delayed but one year he would now surely be his father's assistant, carrying wailing children against their will to the *cheder*. Instead he has just been to America as a representative of a great country, and was returning to the Workers' Fatherland.

In the telling, he let slip the fact that he had taken a German ship to America.

"On a German ship?" I asked in astonishment. It cut me to the quick, but he spoke of it with such steely indifference that I actually envied him. Behold an emancipated Jew! The father a *melamed* in a small Polish village, and the son, in the Hitler period,

63

traveling unconcernedly on a German ship!

"The food was tasty," he said with evident relish, "and we did not discuss politics. They were careful and we even more so."

"But how does a Jew feel on a German ship nowadays?"

He looked at me with a pitying smile.

"You ask a sentimental question and we have no time for sentimentality."

Again I envied my liberated brother and asked him to join me in a toast to the new Jew, who did not respond sympathetically in Moscow when Jews were beaten in Algeria.

"A toast to the new Jew!" I shouted masochistically.

"Sentimentality again," he retorted. "Let's drink to the New Man!"

And he began to describe the idyl of a day in Soviet Russia. One works hard, but for whom? For oneself, of course. If one works very hard and demonstrates ability, he is entitled to vacations, trips; special theatrical performances, ballets, reserved seats at the movies; sanitaria and free medical treatment. And if any one wishes to strive even harder, he gets paid for every bit of work. He, for example, after a day in the factory, is an evening lecturer in the university—for which he is paid—and when he is not in the university, he frequently drops in at the factory late in the evening to work at some plan. The foundation of the Soviet Union is work, but it is sweet because one labors for himself.

"There are some who earn so much that they can't spend all their money, so they save up a good many thousands of rubles. But have no fear, there'll be no breeding of millionaires among us. What can you do with money? You help a friend, you give it away, or return it to the government in an indirect way by buying government bonds."

From the ballroom there came to us the dance music and the clip-clop of heavy and light feet on the gently swaying floor. It seemed as if the dancing and music were an accompaniment to the idyl of Soviet life described to me.

"You know, I'm not sure I'll be able to make myself clear," I began. "I come from Lublin, a small town. I remember the

64

revolutionary songs our workers used to sing. How they hoped for the social revolution! They literally wept it into being with their tear-stained, red-rimmed eyes. They sought equality—equality with Rothschild, and with our town magnate.

"But life is like a filthy midwife at delivery, crushing this one's skull, that one's hands, another's feet—the devil knows from what accursed age-old sources or ancestors it stems—while patting someone else on the head and dangling a little red cordon from his neck.

"So *one* grows up with a glib tongue, while the other never learns the secret of combining words and is enslaved to all who can tell him more fluently what he desires or should desire. One has gifted hands; the other's are awkward. One is born with a dull brain; the other with a brilliant mind and a penchant for mathematics. So decrees the despotism of tens of thousands of dark years and great-great-grandmothers and grandfathers, aunts and uncles, and the devil knows what other genetic secrets from Cro-Magnon or Neanderthal times.

"And you Bolsheviks play into the hands of this filthy midwife. You accept her decrees. You reward competency; and the helpless, accursed, and unfortunate incompetency remains without compensation. Talent drinks Caucasian wine; ineptitude barely gets some stale bread. The heavy-hearted tailors and cobblers with their tearful thoughts have not gotten anywheres yet. Where are they, those pleasure ships that were supposed to course the seas with hundreds of thousands of just such trouble-ridden unfortunates? When will their day come? Where is the recompense particularly for their helplessness? Their tearful stammering words have won the revolution for you wise, intelligent—and believe me that I mean it sincerely—truly fine engineers!

"Take your comrade here—he had to win a lottery in order to achieve equality with your capabilities, in order to get a year's rest. He had no other choice—neither capitalism nor bolshevism wishes to pay for his ineptitude. He isn't shrewd, can't play politics, can't make speeches; he's no brilliant mathematician. But *he* has really helped build the New Life, and not merely for the

65

cultured, talented young men and lucky fellows who hop on the wagon and promptly have the reins in their hands."

All of us were walking on deck now. The night was clear enough to count pearls. From the ocean a refreshing and invigorating breeze blew.

My companion put his hand on my shoulder in a friendly manner, "You're a sentimental bourgeois and an enemy of the Soviet Union," he said, "and I just don't understand what you're babbling."

A ship with small lights caught up with our liner and began to escort it.

Sonya Yakovlyevna danced with joy, exactly like a Robinson Crusoe sighting sudden rescue. Chazhev and the tall American schoolmistress were leaning on the ship's rail and looking toward the twinkling lights of our escort. The Finnish woman was singing a Finnish folksong; the woman from Riga kept reciting verses from sea ballads in five or six languages. The middle-aged Englishwoman, who was walking arm in arm with the blond Russian and kept lagging behind with him in some corner, whispered into my ear with her hot breath after each such concealment:

"Aren't these Russians just exquisite!"

VI

On deck there was so much sunshine that it seemed as if everyone were enveloped in a thin cellophane-like sheath of it. Suits, dresses, stockings, and eyes appeared warmer, brighter, and more transparent. The little hairs on the women's bare legs, which were extended on the deckchairs as if on display, quivered in the sunshine like tiny blades of grass. The fluttering hairs glittered endearingly like specks in the comet-like tail of dust raised by a broom in a sun-drenched room.

A physician whose acquaintance I had made nabbed me at last after a search of several days. He motioned his wife to be on her way, and immediately started to explain in great detail how he had found a cure for the incurable Addison's disease.

He divided his practice between America and Europe, which had once meant Germany, but now, he said with a sigh, that was taboo. So he was bound for a physicians' convention in Austria to disclose his cure for Addison's disease.

In his grotesque English he told me that in general doctors were really—here followed a slightly vulgar word, which he seemed to enjoy using. He paused to see what impression it had made, and whether I sensed how far from wise his professional colleagues were.

At this point he digressed a little to lecture me on how frugal one must be with women: flirt, jest, play the fool—why not? But do not dissipate your strength! Learn to get pleasure from life and to be thrifty—it is no inexhaustible fount!

"A great doctor is telling you this and not a mere little M.D. who is—you already know what."

But he did not risk being misunderstood and again informed me what doctors are. His wife had come up and he also shared the information with her—let her enjoy it too! She smiled in embarrassment and continued on her way.

The Lithuanian woman passed by and greeted me. I introduced the doctor, who immediately availed himself of the opportunity to promenade over her with his hands, under the pretense that she had a beautiful neck, a healthy skin, a finely developed bust, a truly shapely back. His plump little hands took liberties until she realized that this was something beyond a physician's examination and excused herself.

"Well, I've just given you a demonstration. I can't say I didn't get any pleasure from a pat here and a pat there, but the main thing is to bear yourself like a man and to preserve the fount of energy."

He explained that the most fatal error doctors make is to speak of different diseases. "The truth is that there are no specific diseases. People are divided into groups—the healthy and the sick. It's that elementary. But doctors have muddled it with complicated theories. A healthy person has all ailments, but dominates them, keeps his organs in harmony. He sets a rhythm to his life. In a sick person all his so-called ailments break loose all at once and become the masters of the situation. There is no such thing as cancer alone. When a person is ill he has a susceptibility to cancer, is on the verge of becoming consumptive, is ready to die of pneumonia—he has everything the good book lists. A doctor, a—you know what I mean, feels for and digs up an individual ailment. What a stroke of luck! A diagnosis! He immediately bombards this ailment with medicinal trash and overlooks the entire field, the human body. Such technique is like an amateur's artistic efforts. It has nothing to do with life and isn't human. He gropes in the dark for an ailment and in the process overlooks the ailing person in whom everything has gotten out of control. He, the little doctor, does not understand that he is dealing with homeostasis and disharmony. He applies the stethoscope, listens to the heart—do you know just what a heart is? Neither does that doctor. You might as well be whistling into his ears. When you listen carefully to the heart you hear—how shall I express it—a Wagnerian opera. Now it pumps victoriously as at the ride of the Valkyries on celestial hoofs, and now the sound turns pianissimo—*Liebestod!*"

He dragged me off to one side and withdrew a pamphlet from his pocket.

"Here, I'll read you a lecture that I gave in 1900. At that time it created a furor in the entire medical world and immediately placed me in the front ranks of the greatest medical men of our generation. Why do I want to read this to you? Because I wish to show you that medicine is the most sublime poetry. First listen to the cadence and beat of words that are already classic:

> She walks in beauty, like the night
> Of cloudless climes and starry skies;
> And all that's best of dark and bright
> Meet in her aspect and her eyes. . . .

"Every school boy knows that that's poetry—

> She walks in beauty, like the night. . . ."

He stressed the accented, and mumbled the unaccented syllables, and tapped while so doing.

"Keep in mind that same rhythm and that same music and you'll see that they were the foundation of my medical paper. Now remember:

> And *all* that's *best* of *dark* and *bright*. . . .

listen closely."

69

He became a completely different individual. His eyes were clouded windowpanes in a rain. The coarse face became a little gentler. His foot beat time. His face flushed with a mixed emotion of pride and bashfulness. He looked like a provincial author reading a work into which he had put his very soul.

The Byronic enchantment of his poetic model had long since vanished, but he was still chanting his monograph. He sang out the long medical terms that identify all kinds of ugly and loathsome diseases of the blood, skin, stomach, and liver, while his feet wove a dancelike pattern, as if the words were dream-language or pantomime material for a dance.

After an hour's declamation, he returned the brochure to his breast pocket with the explanation that he had merely wished to show me what medicine was.

"Medicine is mystery, intuition, music, poetry. Of course, only if it is practiced by a doctor and not by a—"

His fleshy lips popped open and again his beloved word tumbled out. He yelled the word again and again, in order to be absolutely certain that everyone could hear it.

At this point the doctor's wife came up. Like a small child he permitted himself to be led away.

The Bessarabian Jew from Bogota was delighted to see me. He had been looking for me unsuccessfully for several days.

Where was I keeping myself? With men or with *shiksas*? Oh, those *shiksas*! "You see that young one there, that bare-legged one who is knitting? Try as you will, you can't get her to look at you. From the very first day I've been hanging around her. And do you think I'm the only one? A whole pack of hungry wolves! But she doesn't spare anyone a glance. And you think maybe the crafty wench, poor little thing, doesn't know that she is being stared at? Far from it. She thrives on it. She loves it. And does it occur to you maybe that she is a ravishing beauty? Nothing of the sort! This creature is as far from what is ordinarily referred to as a beauty as I am far from Bogota at present. Skin and bones and snaky legs. You see how they curl and uncurl, how she entwines one leg around the other and then unwinds it—knows all the kittenish tricks. Even has shadows under her eyes from so many sinful thoughts. Don't worry, I'm a connoisseur of such things. I'm ready to bet that all these beauties that you read about in history and storybooks, those who thoroughly drained the men, were scarcely beauties—the beautiful Helens, the Cleopatras, were skinny wretches just like this little *shiksa*. Cruel things who stored within themselves hell-fire, fire upon fire, who begrudged you a smile because you might enjoy it and she might find pleasure in it. Burned night and day, until they finally snared just the fool *they* desired, and woe to him! With such a chap they settle accounts for all time, and consume him to a cinder. You think I don't know that you have to steer clear of such witches and flee as far as your legs will carry you? But go run, when it's the third day that I'm hanging around the little *shiksa* like a ninny, and believe me, she would sooner notice me if I was an onion or a radish. So keep well. I'll keep hanging around awhile. It's quite useless and effort in vain, but maybe something will come of it yet."

Not far from me a heated discussion about books was going on, and since my well-known Danish friend was one of the participants, he employed all sorts of stratagems to involve me too. He directed phrases at me and set snares for my capture, but I resisted with all my powers.

An emaciated young man with a small narrow head was holding forth as an expert on the American book industry, authors, Greenwich Village, and about his brother who had been swallowed up in the village and whose permanent occupation was professional nonconformist. He had been an anarchist, a member of the IWW, a Socialist, a Communist, and now ultimately is a homosexual.

Several days ago the Scandinavian had imparted to me the fullest details concerning the emancipated young man—first of all, that he was not as young as he appeared, that he was loaded with years and money, that he was the president of an old American publishing house, inherited from his father and grandfather, which published college and high school textbooks. This young fellow, the Scandinavian told me, had been divorced twice, and had two children with each wife. Now he was on vacation for the first time in twelve years. He was traveling to Germany to familiarize himself with their book-publishing methods and to establish business connections. During the entire trip he kept sending radiograms to his firm, because he felt uneasy at having left the business in alien hands, and he was a man who loved to work hard himself as well as to see that others were driving themselves.

In addition to this information, I myself knew the publisher to be something of a Dr. Jekyll and Mr. Hyde. He would spend the entire day with men, not even glancing at a woman; but at night he would spruce up and go to the ballroom, where he kept dragging girls to the bar and from there to the darkest nooks on deck. At night he would suddenly become myopic as far as men were concerned. He literally did not recognize any of the friends with whom he had been recently passing the time so pleasantly. However, in the daytime he no longer recognized any of the women. He did not even greet them. He kept two sets of ledgers: the day was for thinking and sharpening one's wits, and the night for lovemaking.

The group around the publisher kept growing, and the Scandinavian still could not bear to see me standing at a distance. He had not given up hope of drawing me into the general discussion. In a final strategic move to conquer, he focused everyone's attention on me with an exclamation:

"Careful! No nonsense now! There's an author nearby; he's eavesdropping, and will write us all up."

The Scandinavian had won. It would have been very rude of me not to join the circle now. However, I obstinately remained no more than a phlegmatic listener. The publisher began to calm everyone.

"We don't fear any authors here. On the ocean we're not people, and therefore an author isn't an author. The sea has immunized us against an author's onslaughts. An author must have characters and we are merely passengers—an altogether different category. We're all without atmosphere here, and characters require background. The ocean is background only for sailors.

72

What can a writer do with us here? How'll he weave us into his plot? How'll he create encounters, conflicts among us, when we are supercautious not to step on one another's toes? What sort of problems can he wish on us, when we are all without problems? But most important is the fact that our meeting isn't prearranged but so damned coincidental. We're all traveling together on the Olympic by chance. However, nothing unites us. If we cared to we might pretend that we are the last generation, without morals or roots, with merely a common hidden fear: should the ship sink, one fate would unite us—common extermination. But that's old and trite and I hardly believe an author would dare touch a theme like that."

All wished to hear what I had to say to this, but quite unexpectedly I was saved by an abrupt change in topic.

One of the group, a principal of a Western high school—a man with large, tobacco-stained teeth, prominent jaw, and a powerful fist that he balled for emphasis—declared categorically that authors were comparable to venomous snakes.

"They're the vilest and lowest members of society!" he cried. "They should be kept in iron cages. Their creations belong to the people, but they—psychopaths and maniacs—should be segregated from society. Writing," he expounded further, "is the most egocentric of professions, and egocentrics are mental invalids with low morals. You have to beware of them."

The Dane explained in an aside that the principal's wife had run off with an author.

The principal had outspoken opinions not only about writers, but about New York and its inhabitants as well.

"New Yorkers are a poisonous race. Once I was in New York for several days, and it was a nightmare. It's a city of pirates. Your wife isn't safe when you pass by with her on Broadway. Even those with their own women seem to want only yours at that moment. It's a pornographic and disgusting city!"

The group around the storming principal was joined by a dentist traveling to Russia to study the problem of hygiene there. He spoke a guttural English. He was a specialist, with an office on Park Avenue and elite for clientele. He claimed he was not

73

traveling first class because he was a democrat. At one time he had been thoroughly at home in the East Side, but that was forty years ago, almost like a dream.

The dentist defended New York against the attacks of the principal, who stated that his stay in New York last time was just long enough to go from train to ship.

"You're all jealous of New York," said the dentist. "That's why you're angry. New York is a city of culture—is in fact the only cosmopolis in the United States. New York is a city of freedom."

"Sure," the principal exclaimed, "that's all you're concerned with: freedom. The freedom of the American Constitution isn't enough for you. Congress, the Senate, the Supreme Court—that's not enough freedom for you. You need still more freedom! Out with it, let's hear it—your Bolshevism, Lenin, Marx, Stalin, and the other saints of the materialistic church!" His enunciation of the last few words with a Yiddish inflection seemed to frighten the dentist.

"Roosevelt saved the country from Bolshevism," the Scandinavian interjected. "When he took office the country was ready for revolution."

"Nonsense! That's what all immigrants think. If you knew all of the United States, you'd know that we don't give a hoot for your revolution. Our revolution is the ballot box. If you don't like the administration, take a big broom and sweep it out; but it must be a constitutional broom. When you New Yorkers try to export your products, Socialism and Communism, to us, we say to hell with 'em!'"

From that the conversation turned to Hitler. A Dr. Schwarz, a Christian of German descent and a native of Milwaukee, suddenly exclaimed:

"To hell with Hitler!"

"Young man," the principal spoke to him paternally, "we don't want and don't need a Hitler here, but we must understand Germany. Hitler is a great leader. He saved the German people from Bolshevism."

74

A pious-faced woman who had joined us unobtrusively began to remind the principal of the crimes committed by the Nazis against the Jews, the forebears of Jesus.

"How unchristian it is! My God, the people of the Bible!"

"Bosh! one just can't recompense the Jews for the Bible!" thundered the principal. "My Bible's the American Constitution, and I say this: according to the Constitution no one can stop me from hating the Jews. But as an American I draw the line between passive hate, as I would call it, and active hate. I'm against pogroms, but I have the right to hate."

"No, you have no right to hate even passively!" shouted Dr. Schwarz. "You poison the world with your hatred. You reek with it! Hatred of Negroes, the yellow race, Catholics, Protestants, Jews—passive in you because your're a school principal—becomes active in the truck driver. You use catchy phrases, you keep quoting the Constitution. No doubt if a Hitler were to appear here, you'd make him constitutional too! He'll swallow your Constitution and crap it on your heads and you'll all cry '*Heil!*' You're worse than syphilitics with your hatred. You're disgusting!"

The respect for the principal crashed suddenly and everybody applauded the young doctor, whose cheeks flushed angrily. He was breathing heavily, and it was evident that he was not a healthy person. His hands were shaking, and the thin, finely chiseled nose quivered. His lips too were still trembling, not having recovered yet from his fiery retort. The applause was prolonged. The lady present actually burst into sobs.

"*That's* America!" The dentist suddenly took courage. "*This* is the voice of America!"

"Young man," the principal said in a subdued tone, "you have a right to your opinion, but—"

Dr. Schwarz walked off hastily and stopped at the railing. He leaned over and tossed scraps of a torn letter into the ocean. The group slowly dispersed. The principal's tone became softer and he strove to retain at least the last of the group, the Scandinavian. But the latter rode rough-shod over him with the admonition:

"You ought to get a radical education. That's your trouble."

More mildly now, the principal developed his notion that it was a struggle of ideas: America against New York—New York at the threshold of Ellis Island and smelling of the foreign; and America with its young indigenous culture.

"But," shouted the Scandinavian, "you ignore completely the economic causes. You should read Bebel's—"

"To hell with Bebel! Jefferson's good enough for me!" exclaimed the principal, and was the first to run at the sound of the copper tray signaling the call to luncheon.

The luncheon was greasy, spicy, salty, and sweet. Even in the cooked state, the fish and meats tasted of the ice which had kept them unspoiled. When the metal platters were uncovered in the dining room, one's head spun from the smell. Later, after several turns around the deck, the greasy, tart, and salty flavors returned with the flatus.

I stood at the rail to let the breeze, stirred up by the choppy, foaming sea, whip about me.

"The best thing's a brandy after meals," the tall pianist remarked when he discovered me at the railing.

The pianist had been avoiding me as well as the other passengers. In the daytime he strolled on deck with a book in his hand, though no one ever saw him reading it. At night, in the saloon, while others wrote letters, read, played chess or bridge, he sat at the piano and played only Chopin.

He was tall and well built, but at the piano he sat hunched up, his head almost touching the keys. The piece ended, he would straighten up to his full height and silently leave for the bar, to sit alone, with his head close to his glass, in the same pose as at the piano.

Usually he strode around the deck, but appeared siesta-minded now. He was even smiling and in a cheerful mood.

"Journey's end!" he said, and repeated this several times, to make sure that I realized that he was punning on the title of the war play. Then his face clouded and the smile disappeared.

"You Americans only saw the war on the stage or in the movies. You joined up when everything was over. The Hun was dead when you were kidded into shooting the final bullet into him—but you've convinced yourselves that you actually finished off Kaiser Bill. We lived through the war. We absorbed the bloody stench into our beings and it'll take a good many years before we get rid of it."

He gesticulated with large, finely shaped hands that were slightly too hairy in contrast to his almost girlish countenance. Even his fingers bore tiny mounds of golden-blond hair. His face was flushed from the liquor he had imbibed, but his legs were steady as he strolled beside me. I learned that he had come to New York five or six years ago. The press had lauded his playing of Chopin. He had been lionized at aristocratic homes.

Life had become unbearable. He met only women.

"Musically inclined women are insane, hysterical creatures! Lord! how do so many middle-aged women happen to be in one city?"

He was seduced day and night and offered no resistance. He tried to, but it was a Ghandi-like passive type. In wealthy New York homes it is always warm—shut windows, heavy drapes, smoke from milady's long cigarettes, sweetish odor of cosmetics and perspiration, bellies and backs on the verge of escaping their confines of girdles, laces, and corsets. He was fondled by so many mothers, he felt that he was playing Oedipus daily.

"Do you know what poverty—English poverty—means? If you ever read Arthur Morrison's *Tales of Mean Streets* you probably got some idea of our luxurious pauperism. English poverty is filth, demoralization, humanity in the raw. It's brute man; shrunken stomachs, offal, and muck. I had to trick my parents into giving me a piece of bread. I had to outsmart my father and get up before him in order to devour the soured leftovers of pigs' knuckles—and catch a whipping later.

"I was too young to go to war, but I did my share, even wore a lousy torn uniform tunic—a shirt was out of the question—slept in barracks; heard the keyed-up, hysterical rejoicing on the eve of

77

departure for the front; saw the half-crazy, savage Tommies come back on leave from 'over there'; saw the truckloads of wounded, crippled, and blinded with glass eyes; heard the macabre music inciting to battle; lay in the cellars for protection against enemy planes.

"I drank. A young rascal, I lay with filthy women and got some food in return. I even stole. I walked barefoot on jagged stones. I became more dog than man, had sly, wolfish eyes on the lookout for food. Then a major's widow took pity on me—she found me in a pub. She was some twenty years older than I. Her husband and an only son had fallen in battle, and I became both to her. My own parents, brothers, and sisters were already a tantalizing dream, and she was a kind woman. When she got drunk, she used to drive me out of the house and shriek that I was a liar, neither her husband nor her son, and that she would shoot me like a dog. But she had kind caressing hands when sober, and at that time I was in need of tenderness. She was a good cook. She hired tutors for me. I began to fill out. Things started clearing up in my head, and finally she reared me into an aristocrat. You can't discover a trace of my lousy parents in me. She even changed my name.

"What's the good of pretense? I'll be frank with you. I've been a gigolo all my life. But when I came to New York it really began to make me sick. My God! They feted and praised me, yet I knew that my heart was scorched to the core. Not only I, but the entire postwar generation. We'll never amount to anything. How can we give the world beauty or even artistic ugliness, if we're thoroughly worm-eaten? Our greatest artist is possibly Joyce. He took Ireland, dressed it in tails and top hat, and let its breeches down. But Joyce was older. During the war years he was already old enough to be an observer, but we were in that damned circle—we saw and heard nothing. The war cast forth dead and dying. The women and the New York critics wanted me to believe that I was a genius. But I knew too well what piano playing meant. Did you ever hear Josef Hofmann?

"So I ran away to Delaware. I now teach music in a wealthy women's university. Women again—that seems to be my fate. But these are young girls who ordinarily become enamored of their teacher and send him anonymous love notes with quotations from Shelley and Keats. It's a small town, and the most beautiful thing about it is its woodland paths. I enjoy horseback riding. Even when a girl is jogging alongside and prattling about Dreiser, Shaw, or Mencken—they still swear by Mencken in Delaware—it doesn't stop me from gazing at the lovely sky."

The Wisconsin schoolmistress was approaching, but before she even had time to greet us, the pianist had excused himself and was gone.

She stopped short and burst into loud laughter that sounded unpleasant and hysterical.

"Why's he always running off? I've been trying to talk to him during the last few days, but he won't let me. Do you realize how handsome he is?"

"But he's an empty husk with neither heart nor lungs."

"Yes, a wonderful robot, dead-tired."

"Then why are you pursuing him?"

"He intrigues me. To thaw out that kind of a person is like warming up one's ears on a frosty day."

"Or like chafing the cold feet of a loved one."

"Exactly! But he's somewhat sinister."

"He hates women. Really hates them."

She sighed. "I wonder how many women he's hated in his time!"

A couple passed us. She was young, pretty, but only when seen in left profile. Full view, she was a different person. Her right eye was blind. A patch over it destroyed the effect of a pretty mouth, lovely head, and the other bright, blue, and frightened eye. Her husband was older than she and quite decrepit. He waddled along on flat feet, as if on crutches. She clutched his arm tightly, while he adoringly pressed close to her. Their affection was touching.

"Maybe it's because the trip is almost over," the teacher remarked, "but I feel depressed. Did you notice that couple? When I think how that half-blind girl grew up carefree and mischievous until her mirror told her clearly that she'd have to make compromises, I feel like crying. I'm sure it's only because the voyage is almost over. I always become depressed because my mind leaps ahead. I see the whole summer before me, and myself at the train, saying good-bye to my new friends and to Parisian liberty. Still another summer gone and myself homeward bound. Every time I travel anywhere, it seems to me that I'm on my way back. Who can tell how many more summers I'll have? And who knows when I'll have no other alternative but to drape myself on an old man for security? Do you know how old I am?"

The pianist scurried by with a book in his hand. She gazed after him longingly.

"Look, let's kill some time and go down to the third class!"

"Fine! An excellent idea! I've some young friends down there, the musicians. They were my first acquaintances aboard ship."

We stood at the companionway leading down to the third class. It was only half a flight, but during the last few days we just stood and gazed at each other as through a telescope. There was little joy below. For us the journey was an aimless one, but one could tell from the haggard, worn faces below that for them the voyage was a torment.

Even from above we could see that the most cheerful group was the orchestra. The young students in their white, summery jackets and dark trousers seemed out of place among the worried passengers.

They greeted me joyfully and, since afternoon tea was being served, invited us to be their very welcome guests.

My companion also thawed out. She began to chat about university life. There followed an exchange of college anecdotes—like all esoteric jokes, utterly dull for outsiders but a source of merriment for intimates.

The students were delighted. This was the first time they had come into intimate contact with a university instructress. The anecdotes began to verge on double-entendre, but the instructress met them on their own ground, which made a real hit with the young men. They laughed loudly—an unrestrained ear-splitting boyish laughter. All restraint collapsed, and it was not long before she was perched atop someone's knee and they were calling her by her first name.

I soon noticed that one of the students was not really laughing, but only pretending gaiety—the way this is sometimes detected at a burlesque show when the entire chorus has come on. They fling their legs, toss their hips, pitch chunks of quivering flesh to the beloved public. A toss to a loge, to someone in the orchestra—even the poor gallery isn't forgotten! One has but to stretch out his hands and catch. The cymbals and the drums are redhot coals underfoot or whips across the body. Out of a clear sky, you notice one of the girls, mimicking all this heaving and wiggling with calisthenic coldness, has become conspicuous in all the hurly-burly. She jerks her body even more violently than the rest, kicks her foot higher than the others, but is merely disrupting the harmony. The more you look at her, the more you notice the mockery.

The student caught my eye, came over and abruptly asked whether I was Jewish.

"Forgive me for asking. I merely wish to know because I'm a Jew and you seem to be too."

"Are you in such great need of a 'brother?' "

He did not answer my question directly, but told me that his father was a doctor in a small town in West Virginia. He had been making a very fine living, until a quiet boycott began, and most of the gentiles were now going to the other doctor in town. Luckily his father put by something for a rainy day and they managed to get along. . . . In the university? The problem doesn't exist yet. Too few Jews, but no matter how few, they are not too well liked.

"Can you perhaps tell me why? My father didn't teach me Hebrew, or Jewish history, or how to pray. He didn't even instill in me a desire to know Jewish history. I know very few Jews, only my parents and several uncles and aunts—all fine people, I must tell you. You're a New Yorker. There are many Jews there. Maybe you can give me the key to this hatred? It's a problem for me."

"There are many keys. You can have your choice. Fit the one that meets your need. There's a national key, there's a Marxist one, there's a masochistic one. Many Jews exaggerate their own failings in order to rationalize the hatred toward them. And don't forget the simple hereditary one—blood, heritage of generations, a child suckles its mother's breast....Are you being treated badly here?"

"Not at all! Excellently! They treat us like princes. We play during the hour after lunch and several hours in the evening. The food is tasty and my colleagues treat me well, at least on the surface. I'm the pianist and the leader."

"That's it! There you've another key, if you wish. You're the leader and they must act properly. That *must* is like a taut string that has to snap. *You* are the leader. Perhaps it's time to let them lead themselves. Let them lead themselves for the next several hundred years and see what they will achieve."

"And what about innate ability? What are you to do if, despite everything, you are a good doctor, a good pianist, a good economist? Must you suppress it within yourself, because the gentiles wish it? What if you're naturally pushed to the head of the row because of your capabilities?"

"So this key isn't to your liking? Well, you'll find another."

Two middle-aged women came over to the table and sat down to drink tea. One was wearing a large black crucifix. Both had yellowish faces, gnarled hands that looked like old branches, and even their feet appeared misshapen and crooked. Their shoes bulged with bunions, corns, and the usual orthopedic ailments. Hands, neck, and face were clean, with the thick skin discolored by a deeply imbedded grime from years of washing clothes, scrubbing, cooking, and household toil.

They were conversing in Polish. I left my Jewish "brother" and his problem, and directed several friendly remarks to them. The one with the cross did not answer at all. The other did respond, but with some misgiving. I gained her confidence, however, when she learned that we were both traveling to visit parents in Poland. She was bound for some place in Galicia, which was now Polish

82

soil. Her parents were very old and poor. Their hut was about to collapse—the rain poured in. She was bringing them some money to repair the shack or perhaps build a new one if possible.

"Are you homesick for Poland?"

"I have grown-up children in America. No, I'm not homesick."

She did not even yearn for the Pennsylvania village where her husband and two sons worked in a coal mine. She was altogether too work-worn and weary to spend time in pining.

The one with the crucifix suddenly burst into tears and sobbing.

Her companion told me that the woman's husband had been killed in a mine accident a few years ago. An only son supported her. He was a strong handsome lad who refused to get married because he did not want to leave his mother. She too was bound for some place in Galicia. An uncle had left her a legacy amounting to several hundred dollars in American money.

It was almost suppertime, but the university instructress was loath to leave the students. They promised to sneak up to join us late in the evening and spend the last night on our deck.

I could not forget the tables, chairs, and floors in the third-class section. Everything was clean and tidy, but like in an institution. True, there was no trace of that penury of a hell hole once called the immigrant 'tween-decks, which I myself had not experienced but had heard described by earlier immigrants. However, every moment that I sat there, I kept expecting a door to open and someone to stick out his head and shake it in refusal. The answer would stun us. With a feeling of doom, we would all rise from the wooden benches . . . .

The two Polish women would rise, the crippled, misshapen feet barely able to support the weight of the broad buttocks and heavy, flattened breasts. They were the kind of heavy, tired feet that are the first parts of the work-worn body to succumb. Toes twist one over the other. The little toe, lacking a nail, curls over the second one; the second imbeds itself into the third, which in time makes a place for its neighbor to lie in comfortably as in a sheath. The exceptionally thick big toe, with a black and blood-clotted nail, protrudes from the side of the shoe and almost bursts through the leather. The shoe is gnarled and shapeless. . . .

Both work-weary women would drop to their knees, to scrub the floors with large brushes dipped into pailsful of soapsuds...

On deck it was quite dark now. The ocean was no longer visible. One had to bend far over the rail to see the white foam shimmering on the dark water, like a mouthful of healthy white teeth in a dark face.

It became damp and I shuddered. And with that shudder there again came to mind my aunt Gnendil's letter about my mother. "Her ears are as yellow as wax. Pack immediately and come; may His Blessed Name grant that you find her alive."

My mother's ears, twenty years ago . . . small ears with tiny holes for earrings. Wee little holes. As a small boy, whenever I thought of how they had taken a long, glowing hatpin to pierce her infant ears, I had to close my eyes and shudder. Her face—earnest, sad, hardly ever a smile—pale but pretty; a bright forehead which became even brighter when my mother removed her peruke. . . . Now these ears were yellow as wax.

Cold despair clamped about my heart. My mother and I, we have lived two decades since that night when she stood in the station in the dark, wringing her hands, waiting for the train which she believed would take me directly to America. Twenty years gone and now at last I was returning home to look at her yellow ears.

My mother had fought against my leaving. She nevertheless had to give in. Father's business had deteriorated with every passing day. It became evident that the day was approaching when we would have to bolt the door and close permanently. Even Ezra, father's partner, began to yield bit by bit. Ezra had a proud, gentile face. His hands trembled with age, his round gray head shook, and the gray, trimmed beard quivered. He could neither read nor write, but considered himself an aristocrat because his second wife was from Lithuania and wore her own hair, and because his son attended the *gymnasium*. He chattered an

84

ungrammatical Polish and Russian, but with clear enunciation. If a tall Russian official or a rich Pole happened to come in he would spring up with alacrity. Gentiles of lesser importance and Jewish customers he left to my father. Generally my father had to serve the patrician customers too, because if someone began to haggle too much, he would become impudent and acidly inquire: "What does the gentleman think, that this is Targ's?" Targ's was the gentile market where second-hand garments were sold for almost nothing.

But even the proud Erza began to hang his head in surrender when queer customers made their appearance in the store—odd individuals, peasants in coarse linen coats, whom he used to chase out like scared hens when they wandered into our store in the good days. "Get out! Beat it! This store isn't for you. I have nothing!"

He himself did not as yet deign to wait on them, but while my father did, pulling the overcoats on and off, Ezra would shut his eyes and heave sigh after sigh, and growl: "A fine old age you've granted me! But what's the use of grumbling, Lord of the Universe!"

It was at the time when the Poles were beginning to avenge themselves against the Jews for helping to elect to the Duma the labor deputy Yagelon, instead of an outspoken anti-Semite whom they preferred. The boycott began in jest, but soon bit deeply into Jewish trade. Stores stopped doing business. Even the Chazanov establishment saw days when not a ruble's worth was sold. The bills came due. Father tried to save himself with advertisements in the Polish newspaper *Zhemya Lubelska*. The *Polyak-katholik* reprinted father's ad and in a sensational editorial reproached its neighbor the *Zhemya* for accepting Jewish advertisements.

My steamship ticket was already in a tin box in the bureau. I was counting the months, the weeks. Even my mother began to hasten the journey. She feared that the store would devour the few hundred rubles which had been put by for my expenses.

The last few weeks before my departure—days spent in the Saxony garden with spring blossoming along all the verdant walks—

my comrades and I strolled about with heads held high like the heroes of Hamsun's *Growth of the Soil*. We walked about the streets of Lublin, our cross-eyed artist with one eye as white as the milt of a herring, and just returned from the Krakow Academy; the poet who was in Warsaw not long before and brought back a batch of testimonials; the violinist with a large, massive, dark head—a graduate of the Warsaw Conservatory, who had appeared in *Hazamir*; our "pessimist," the professional cynic and misogynist, with clammy hands and long black nails, the eldest among us, who had delved into the Upanishads, quoted Schopenhauer and Weininger, and boasted that he masturbates purposely rather than have commerce with women; my friend who spent a year and a half at a sister's far off in Ufa and therefore strove to speak with a Siberian accent, throwing in for effect "rather" and "indeed" indiscriminately; and several well-read young men who were planning to be critics and carried around volumes of Taine, St. Beuve, Byelinski, and *our* Brandes most of all.

We strutted about like peacocks and were as unreal as characters out of a novel. These were my Bazarovs, Nyechlodovs, Tidemans, Karamazovs, Oblomovs, Sanins, Hamlets, and Don Quixotes. Around us blazed a gentile life—several: one Polish and the other Russian, at each other's throats—and a Jewish life, in which, worlds apart and separated like castes, were the untouchable paupers and the Jewish aristocrats who rode in carriages drawn by spirited horses. About us the streets teemed with tailors, cobblers, tinsmiths, cigarette-makers, brickyard laborers, sugar-refinery hands, tanners, iron-workers, teachers, water-carriers, servant-girls, stocking-makers, seamstresses, musicians, wig-makers, magnates, *dayonim* and *rabonim*—tribunes of the Jewish court and rabbis—but we saw no one. We dueled with ready phrases and wound our way home to mother for supper and for a few more kopeks spending money.

The poet recited a poem about spring. He had a sad, lilting voice which coddled each rhythmless line. He had been influenced strongly by "Little Ber-Yoskele, pray for me too!" and pleaded

86

with the flowers and the spring zephyrs for a favor—I no longer remember exactly—of some sort.

All of us thought highly of him. We had great hopes for him, believed he would become the boast of the town. Even I, who had already written poetry and stories, thought little of myself in comparison. I envied his melancholy verse, which sounded like poetry even before one had grasped the sense of the words.

The poet's father was wealthy. He lived in a gentile neighborhood, in one of the newest houses, with mirrors in the corridor and divans on the stair landings—one of the houses which, after they had been built, the entire city had gone to inspect out of curiosity; a wonderfully beautiful residence: large salons with mirrors, heavy furniture, blue and red plush chairs, tall vases, cages of singing canaries, a young, kind stepmother who looked like an elder sister of the poet and seemed a part of the entire modern interior. She leaned backward in being good to her "child" and even to his friends. The poet had a wonderfully carved writing desk where he kept his notebook of poems written in a most meticulous script. His first poem, which he read to me in his study, in a tearful voice, was entitled "The Young Mother Is Dead" and was a frank imitation of the melodiousness of "The Old Precentor Has Died." The young poet made no secret of his imitation. On the contrary, he boasted how well he had copied the master and I marveled indeed at his skillful faithfulness to the original. I simply could not understand how, in that atmosphere of comfort, such melancholy and sorrow came to him. I thought that even if he truly were mourning for his mother, nevertheless it was a bit of ingratitude to write such a dirge, with so kind, devoted, attractive, and silent a stepmother present. At that time I was writing patriotic epics and erotic narratives, but I considered myself second-rate in our small literary family, and merely because I envied him God's gift of sorrow when it seemed to me he should have felt happy indeed.

All of us found his spring poem more delightful than the spring. Only our professional cynic had a vulgar word of derision. He cited long passages in Russian from Homer, and in German from

87

Heine, and subjected the poem to a ruthless attack. However, the poem lost not a mite of its worth for us, although we enjoyed his epigrammatic asperity.

My journey was mentioned, and they expressed envy of as well as pity for me, for I was heading for the country of the "yellow press."

At night, once more the sidewalks leading each "class" separately to the Saxon garden: on one walk strolled only laborers and their womenfolk, and on the other, boy and girl students of the *gymnasium*, and officers; again the dark paths along which one ran hungrily after every brown-skirted silhouette of a *gymnasium* pupil.

In the morning I sauntered once more along the field paths and wandered off to the sandy stretch where my Aunt Choma lived in her own cottage, with her own hens, several ducks, and sometimes even a turkey, and with two husky daughters whose bare feet were callused and whose hands always smelled of parsley, onions, and parsnips. The elder one would often drag me off to the railroad quite a distance from the house and even beyond the tracks. There she would gaze into my eyes, breathe on me hotly and sing peasant love songs, but if I showed signs of warming up a bit, her "Yankele, don't!" in a husky, cold voice, sobered me up immediately.

A fortnight before my departure I received some bad tidings which took all the glamour out of my trip. I had been thinking all along that I would not be traveling alone, that is, that I would have a girl companion, and what a shipmate! A year and a half younger than me, she was tall, slender, fair, with a tip-tilted nose. But her brown eyes contrasted so wonderfully with her blond hair that whenever I saw her I could not stop marveling at the warmth of her eyes and the cold look of her hair. Her walk was already that of a woman. She had agile, well-proportioned legs and a rather wide mouth with thin lips, but a sweet smile which, worked like a bold wink, compensated for the mouth.

She was of a common family, all butchers, and butcher's helpers. Her parents, uncles, aunts had red hands with long, blood-stained nails, red faces, heavy feet, coarse voices, but she herself seemed noble, delicate. Her smile was perhaps the heritage of generations of knowing and getting what one wishes, but on her lips it gave the effect of a vulgar expression transformed into a refined warning and with a "Pardon me!" added.

They were our neighbors on the new road, where we lived opposite the gentile and Jewish meat markets, which displayed oxen and calves-heads with gentle, open, dead, velvety eyes. Even the family name, or as it was known among us, the German name of her family, suggested the butcher.

At that time many Jewish girl students in our city were greatly influenced by Tolstoyan morality, and before one earned a kiss he had to wade through long quotations of the New Testament. "And he who gazes on a woman with lust has already sinned with her in his heart." One had to preach long before one could sin, and to sin meant to hold her hand, gaze into her eyes, and recite from Nadson in the dark. What came first in our town, the egg or the hen, the Saninism or Tolstoyism I no longer remember exactly, but both swung like swords about the Garden of Eden as two distinct sets of morals. Sometimes one had to play a worldly-wise Sanin with his "Seize-the-present" and sometimes Tolstoy with his "Prepare for the heavenly kingdom."

And when playing at morality became boring, one abandoned some of his dignity and made the acquaintance of a seamstress or stocking-maker. True, their fingers were bruised and chapped but they sang heart-rending Jewish folksongs or Goldfaden ballads and had warm hands that could hug tightly. All they pleaded was, "Fear God and respect people's gossip!" Everything else came joyfully from two young people, and one did not have to babble entire chapters from the New Testament first.

My mother knew that I was interested in the butcher's little daughter and took no pleasure in the fact. She feared a match and it was not at all to her liking, because in addition to everything else there was a skeleton in the closet. Her cousin had been converted and had married a *shegitz*, a butcher's helper, and to mortify her parents had opened a gentile meat ship close to theirs. Her parents went about red-faced and ashamed to look anyone in the eye. And the daughter, the proselyte, was now pregnant and was selling pork with remarkable dexterity.

My mother was afraid that I was about to land in the midst of such a family. At that time I had exchanged perhaps ten or a dozen words with the girl. However, I went hot when I learned suddenly that she was to travel together with me to America, to her uncle. (Her mother knew that in Lublin the family skeleton would haunt her constantly.) We would travel together on the train, aboard ship, as well as disembark in Castle Garden together. Her mother was happy that her daughter would be with an acquaintance, a respectable youth who would take care of her.

But something came up. For me it was a real misfortune, as she had to leave two weeks ahead of me. The blow came unexpectedly. She met me in town and with a smile explained, "Y'know, I'm leaving tomorrow." Neither from her voice nor expression could I tell whether it was as much of a blow to her as it was to me. It hurt me doubly. I felt myself alone, and suddenly the long, lonely trip I had to take became frightening. She extended her hand with its long, pointed fingers: "I'll see you in New York."

That night I felt as if a wife had left me.

The longest trips I ever dared take alone were from Lublin to Warsaw, to my Aunt Gnendel. But my grandfather showed me the way several times.

I first began to travel alone after my grandfather's death. I ordinarily rode fourth class with him. The train crawled and crawled and seemed to take pains to stretch a four- or five-hour trip into a full twelve hours. We would start out in broad daylight and arrive past midnight.

Even in the fourth class where a ticket cost next to nothing, the passengers would haggle with the conductor. My heart used to bleed at seeing tall, full-bearded, dignified Jews, Jews capable of landing a solid blow, hiding under the benches, backsides uppermost as when receiving the penitential flogging on the day before Yom Kippur in the synagogue. Whenever an inspector got on, these Jews would be dragged out from under the seats and thrown off at a station.

Amid all this misery in the fourth class roamed men with punchboards and picks, and card players seeking an idle coin.

My grandfather had a fine habit. He would untie his kerchief and refresh himself with a hardboiled egg, a chunk of bread, a Hungarian free-stone plum, and a golden-yellow pear that spurted juice all over his beard, and meanwhile reproach me: Why did he have to take along a rascal like myself to shake the hand of the Hafetz Chaim, the great rabbi? And why did he have to spend a half *kerbel* for a book if I never even opened it? Grandfather, however, was not angry. He carried on the entire monologue for pleasure's sake, because "you have to say something before falling asleep." Then he would begin to snore in his beard.

I would drink in masses of fields, trees, forests, streams which the train was devouring slowly and pantingly. At night the passengers would stretch out on all the benches and even under them. Only the conductor with his smoky lantern and his "Have your ticket?" would disturb the stillness.

A handsome young fellow with a small black mustache, patent-leather boot tops, and a shiny visor lies with nose pressed to the dark window and hums a woeful ditty. Heads rise from all sides—feet in rags stomp, and there are shouts of "Quiet!"—but when they see the type of passenger it is, turn over on the other side, sigh and groan, "Oh, Father in Heaven!" as if to say, "What creatures you've put on this little world! But we dare not say a word!"

The young fellow, who looks like a pander, sings with his nose pressed to the window:

> Oh, Feige darling, Feige dear,
> Take the reward of merit,
> Take the reward of merit.
> When I bid you prepare the bed,
> You've no reason at all to fear.

When I bid you prepare the bed,
You've no reason at all to fear.

Several taps on the windowpane with his fingers and he gives
Feige dear's reply in a thin, sweet, heartrending voice:

Done, done, the bed is done,
But with whom am I to dally?
With whom am I to dally?
For so low and common a fellow
A wanton to become?
For so low and common a fellow
A wanton to become?

Tra-la. The rails dance and leap from under the wheels to the
same tune and with the same wretched refrain of the window: "A
wanton to become."

The young man continues his singing, tapping on the window
several times, while pausing to change to the woman's voice. He
ladles out the song to its very end, from the going to bed, to
Feige dear's inevitable last sad refrain, "A wanton to become."

Such a liberated Feige dear probably shows up later in our own
Lublin, to hover around the town clock with shawl over head,
jangling her keys.

The lamps over the Weissel bridge begin to appear. They seem
to be neither fixed nor of metal, as they dip in and out of the
Weissel. . . . Many little red, green lamps; then the Warsaw station.

Grandfather and I grope our way in the dark along several
blocks to a gateway. We pull the rusty bell and wait, wait until
the clack of sabots on stone resounds, then an oath that is
silenced by grandfather's coin. Grandfather leads me by the hand
through a long courtyard, up steps, and knocks. My aunt opens
the door, kisses me with soured mouth—because its sleep had been
disturbed—tumbles me into a bed, covers me with a heavy
comforter, and I can hardly fall asleep for delight at having

experienced a train ride and at being about to drowse off in a strange city, far from home.

In the morning I orient myself and inspect the great "wonders" of the new city. First, a hallway water closet, a dark one with black, peeling walls, but nevertheless, a water closet which gurgles but does not flush. A large yard with entrances on four or five sides. The yard smells of tar, plaster, sewer, malodorous white disinfectant, and urine. A kitchen gas stove in my aunt's apartment reeked of an overwhelming odor like that of cheap fresh paint or kerosene rubbed into braids as a remedy for nits. The pipe apparently has a slight leak, but it occurs to no one that it should be repaired.

My uncle, a dealer in oxen, knows that he has to bring home some tripe from the slaughterhouse, because about fifty years ago in Lublin, as a result of a dispute with a meat supervisor, a rabbi of blessed memory had proscribed tripe. The prohibition remains in force in our town to this very day, but elsewhere a Lubliner may eat as much tripe as his heart desires. Although I do not relish the tough morsels that chew like goose skin and curl up like the pages of a prayerbook, I nevertheless eat with gusto. I feel that I am in a strange city where I am allowed to eat something that is almost *trefeh*, ritually unclean, but which has become kosher because I took a train and rode for miles.

In honor of the guest, my uncle also brings home some udder, a delicacy calling for special preparation in a little earthen pot that is destroyed immediately after use, because udder is a sort of meat-in-milk. My mother never wanted, on any account, to venture into the experiment of preparing udder, but my uncle desires to show me Warsaw with all its wonders. I also eat udder with special interest because I desire to taste the forbidden drop of milk-in-meat.

The night's unique nocturne—the mournful clatter of streetcar with cheap wooden benches and worn plush seats for the segregation of the populace—five-kopek plebeians from the seven-kopek aristocrats ... the wooden omnibuses bumping over the cobbles and seeming momentarily about to collapse like barrels into firewood . . . large, lighted lamps that look like heavy-laden, slender trees . . .the promenade to and fro on Vilenska Street . . . the flirtation with the *gymnasium* students in the yard . . . young Tyomkina, a slim, freckled girl with thin legs and wiry, strong little hands, plain face, but with a lovely mouth that kisses delightfully in the dark as she twists out of my arms and has the nerve to wish me a "peaceful night". . . .

The train ride back . . . floating lamps that dance in the distance . . . long dark stretches . . . a woeful whistling in the night . . . the sun turning the window rosy . . . a sun above a barren field, a village sun with dairy products, sour milk, noodles with cinnamon and cheese . . . a cow that lazily raises its head toward the rushing train, hesitates and does not moo . . . the rails dancing "Done, done, the bed is done, a wanton to become, become" . . . Tyomkina's little hot hands . . . peaceful night. . . . Whoa—as if the train had lurched into a slight dip but had immediately recovered. Apparently I had just dozed off, because there had not as yet been enough action in the dream, merely unraveled possibilities. . . .

I bite my younger sister and am off for the station . . .before midnight. Everything appears like a soot-blackened lamp . . .everyone seems hunched up as if about to doze off . . . the entire station full of my friends, relatives, young men, girls. I wait for one . . . a year now that we have not been speaking to each other. I could not overcome my stubbornness and persuade myself to bid her good-bye. . . . It would be fine if *she* were to come to say good-bye. Much depends on such a gesture from her, it seems to me . . . just what I do not know exactly. I look for her in the darkness. . . . It grows late . . . I realize that she is not there. . . .

My father pretends indifference and tells a joke. One lip is trembling, almost distorting his mouth. My mother is wringing her hands. The station guard in his red hat comes to meet the puffing train. I am already aboard with my bundles that smell of mother's pastry, raisin cakes, egg cookies. . . .

"What? What?" Yells, farewells, but everything is dark,

sleepy. . . . "What? What?" Deaf, from afar, as when the royal troops are seen off. . . . "What? What?" I hear nothing because the train is already speeding and heaving and puffing as though it were blowing into a fire-pot. . . .

Sosnowitz . . . and by droshke on the way to the smuggler.

"*Sholem aleichem,* young man! What's your name?" He takes out a letter and compares. It checks.

I lie on a hard bench. . . .

At daybreak I make out a large room that resembles a long pantry, and I smell the old wood of the benches and of the long plank tables. A fifteen or sixteen-year-old girl enters on light slippers that are loose and keep slapping and pattering along the floor.

She braids a plait while walking and then tosses it over her shoulder. A pale face, large astonished eyes. The flash of white, half-bared arms, bare feet and neck are enough to evoke a sense of nakedness and temptation.

"Are you the American? Papa is saying his prayers; he'll come in right away."

She hands me a dented copper quart vessel and points toward the barrel of water for me to wash my hands. She brings in hot water with milk and several buttered rolls. Every time he comes close to me I smell the warmth of a bed, or kneaded dough with the sweet-sour aroma of yeast.

"You're to be envied," she says to me with a sigh, and tears well up in her eyes. "You'll be well off in America."

"What are you, a fortuneteller?"

But she does not hear me.

"Of course you're to be envied." She speaks in a forlorn and faraway voice, as far away as her eyes that look toward and beyond the street, all the way to my America.

I stand at the decaying barrel. My face floats about in the black water. I fill the quart and empty it, fill it and empty it. And I recall the wonder story about the Jew who went to Egypt to learn black magic. En route he stops at a caravanserai, and when the

95

innkeeper hears that he is on his way to learn magic, he bids him first to wash before the meal. While the Jew stands thus with the vessel over the barrel, the innkeeper casts a spell over him, and reveals a fantastic life to him. The Jew marries, becomes wealthy, falls into the hands of pirates, is rescued, becomes impoverished, scores of years go by with unusual realism, leaving him unhappy, decrepit, old—and when life is about to flicker out, the innkeeper breaks the spell and the Jew realizes that he has been standing over the barrel of water only a few moments while experiencing a terrifying life.

I imagine that this girl too will soon put a spell over me, and I will remain here all my life. Who cares for America? Who needs to go off on so long a journey? Remain here, marry the smuggler's daughter, wear a satin dressing gown, on the Sabbath sit at the table spread with the savory twist bread, the sweet fish, beans with *ferfel*, a piece of fat meat with horseradish, carrots stewed in rich gravy, plum compote, and the little glass of golden Visotski! The candles in the tall silver candelabrum will flare up and try to avoid going out, and in the quiet darkness I will sleepily kiss my young, bashful, pregnant wife. . . . *Blub-blub*, I see my face floating in the black barrel. . . .

I sit and sip the water with milk while she stands near me. She seems lonely, as only a Jewish maiden can who suddenly grows up before the parents have noticed and try to understand her.

"You're certainly to be envied!"

The smuggler enters in his praying shawl and phylacteries, touches his fingers to the arm phylactery, to the head phylactery, and kisses them.

"Nee-aw," he points to his mouth and says in Hebrew, "had something?"

I show him, also in pantomime, that I had the glass of water and milk.

He *tsk's*, mocks me.

"Rachel," he shouts to his daughter, "nee-aw, a little sour milk! Nee-aw, a scallion! Wench, oh wench!" He points to his head, implying that she has no sense. She slaps about in her slippers and

96

brings me a plate of sour milk.

He touches his phylacteries, as if to ask: have I prayed yet? When he realizes my embarrassment, he quickly exclaims, "Nee-aw, nee-aw!" points to his derriere and up at the ceiling and shakes his head. He is making it very clear to me that he will not be flogged on my account. He abruptly assumes the position for the prayer of eighteen blessings, and is directly moving three paces backward—a sign that he has concluded—as if he were stepping out of a harness. . . .

At nightfall a chap arrives dressed in hip boots, with the tops pulled above his knees. There also appears suddenly a young man who had deserted from the army. He doffs the kaiser's uniform at the smuggler's place and dresses in mufti, even puts on spectacles.

The soldier fidgets as if sitting on hot coals.

"When will we finally get moving? When do we start?" he demands. "You want to kill me here! Do you know what's in store for me?"

The chap in the hip boots is in no rush. First of all he orders a herring and some liquor. He keeps packing in mouthful after mouthful of black bread and pours down one glass after another. After each drink, he tries to calm the soldier.

"Why worry? You're in good hands."

But even the smuggler begins to remind the fellow of his duties.

"Rachmiel, let go of the bottle! Your head. You must have your wits about you."

When it becomes very dark, the smuggler settles accounts with us. He wishes us a pleasant journey, reminds the fellow to keep his head on his shoulders.

"Depart in peace! Depart in peace!" he utters with a devout ministerial air. The girl is suddenly at my side. She proffers a cold hand and I search for a kind word, but my tongue merely stutters.

"Will we ever get started? You're slaughtering me! I'll have to put a rope around my neck!" The soldier begins to lament like a woman.

"Depart in peace! Depart in peace!"

The girl flees like a kitten to the farthest corner. The fellow pulls the door wide open and we step into the darkness.

"Rachmiel!" the smuggler yells after him, "remember, woe to your bones! Keep your head!"

We pass through back streets. In the distance we hear a dog barking. It is a dark night and we tread on soft earth with springy steps. The fellow in the boots walks ahead and reels a bit. He mumbles to himself.

"He gives me the head of a herring, a taste of *aquavit*, and half a ruble, and thinks he's making me rich, that cutthroat! To blazes with him!"

The soldier keeps blabbering that should the attempt fail, God forbid, he will do away with himself. We walk and walk and do not look at one another. Suddenly things begin to transpire as in a fairy tale. First the leader in the hip boots disappears. Later when I cast a sideward glance, the soldier has also disappeared. I begin to walk more quickly, imagining that I am the victim of a ruse, that I have been duped of my money and have been left stranded between somber sky and dark earth. I hurry even more, and in great fright stride on with firm step and head high, as is often the way with one on the verge of a crack-up.

Soon the muddy paths change into clean narrow sidewalks. I continue in the same direction. Tidy little houses appear with an occasional lighted window, and suddenly I am in the center of a town, among wagons and trams that run by with a *whoosh*. The same gentile faces, gentile mustaches, and gentile mouths as in every Polish town, but the surprise comes when they open their mouths. I look at each peasant face and cannot stop marveling—the mouth opens and I hear *"Ja, ja."*

I approach a policeman who looks like one of our constables, even before I am close to him, he greets me: "At your service!"

I mix with the people on the street and begin to rouse myself as from a dream. *Ja, ja*, safely across the border. *Ja, ja*. A change in geography had taken place. No bells have chimed and no cannons have roared, but simply crossed from *pshakrev†* to *ja, ja*. I find a strange pleasure in gazing into faces and waiting until the

98

---

† A bitch's offspring (Polish)

mouth opens and—*ja, ja.*

Most of them are slightly drunk. A young peasant pulls me into a smoke-filled bar in an inn. I drink rich, foaming dark beer from a tall, slender mug. They sing, they spit. I hesitate to ask where I am, but by sly means finally discover that the place is Mislivitz and that one can get by trolley directly to Kattovitz. I barely manage to get away from the friendly drunkards and the inn. That same night I am in Kattovitz. . . .

Trains, trains, trains. . . . Hanover, Frankfurt, several hours in Berlin. . . . Riding, riding onward. . . . Trains with merry, singing students in small green hats. . . . I am tired; my head is light from lack of sleep. . . . Not until Bremen am I recognized by my carefree bearing as an immigrant, and then I am no longer my own master. I am subjected to legal control but no longer care because I am dead tired. I see everyone as through the narrow end of a telescope and hear unending words that stretch on like pitch in the summertime and have no coherence whatsoever. . . .

That night I slept on a stone shelf that felt like a step in a cold bathhouse. Each time my face or hand touched the cold stone I awakened. It was pitch dark. Men and women were speaking some kind of incomprehensible Yiddish that seemed to make no sense. Near me lay a woman, breathing into my face. All night her heavy bare foot rested on me and I feared to stir. In the morning I realized that all these "Jews" and "Jewesses" were actually Flemish-speaking non-Jews.

I answered a series of formal questions, took a shower, and before realizing it was on a briny ship that stank of tar, old rope, rusted iron, and disinfectant. Sacks and barrels lay scattered over the entire deck. We were fed coarse food and later everyone subsided into his own private hell. I lay in isolation for a day and a half and felt my intestines exploding through my mouth. I raised a heavy head to seek a sympathetic face, saw myself surrounded by bitter enemies, and became indifferent to the passage of time.

Arrived safely in Halle, all the Jews, male and female, were assembled and a rabbi intoned a blessing over us. He sermonized about nomad people Israel and about Jacob's feet that were weary

99

of wandering. We were served at dark tables between damp walls. My stomach still felt sore from the short sea voyage. With trepidation I crunched some hard bread and listened warily after each bite to make sure that no accident followed. I sipped cold, insipid, turbid tea. . . .

A train . . . Liverpool . . . a free transients hotel with several rooms that were really one, separated from each other merely by steps—several steps down to the right, a roomful of beds; several steps to the left, the dining hall.

I met a young man there. He introduced me to his sister, Lisa, a girl with red hair and freckles, and to her friend Sonya, who toyed with her two long braids, braids so black that they actually seemed wet. The young man struck me as a peculiar individual because he was not going to New York but to Connecticut. He and his sister sang moving Russian love songs. All four of us chatted in Russian and prowled about for three days in the Liverpool streets. . . .

The *Aquitania.* . . . We stood on the deck. The luggage was being hoisted aboard. Big fellows with strong hands were joshing one another as they worked.

Near me on the deck stood a tall man of about sixty, with massive shaven head. The clean-shaven face appeared somewhat hermaphroditic and Edison-like—not a trace of hair to be detected, only rosy little veins that branched over his face like a map.

The man exchanged jests with the agile lads who were loading the baggage on the dock. From the deck he shouted a word at them and they burst into laughter. They answered him and his laughter rolled forth like thunder. I did not understand a word, but absorbed the inflections of the strange tongue.

The tall man with the large head was a German-American who had visited his birthplace and was now returning to America.

Later, on board ship, the German-American got into a conversation with me, good-naturedly poked fun at me and at the Jews in general. "All the Jews," he said, "are emigrating to New York. The whole Jewish folk is going to an uncle, and the uncle works in a shop at shirts, cigars, or pants." He advised me to

100

shove my uncle up my butt and instead to go with him into the country, where he had horses, cows, hogs, and chickens. He would gladly take me along and even pay my traveling expenses from New York to his home. I was still a young man, and did not have to end up in a murky sweatshop. Why shouldn't I live a healthful life?

The German told me about the American prairie, and the clear air for shrunken Jewish lungs, about nights that give one rest, about strange birds that cry *whip-poor-will* all night; and with a lewd wink of an eye at my youthfulness, he also tried to entice me with stories about *shiksas* prowling about in the hay at night.

The Jewish cook with the white chef's cap did not allow the Jewish passengers to forget that it was Shevuoth, the Festival of Pentecost. He prepared excellent dairy dishes and exceptionally fine puddings. I, my friend, and the two girls strolled about the deck until late at night, singing Russian songs. Lisa was a slightly anemic girl and went to bed before we did, but the dark Sonya had a wiry endurance. She kissed me and my ship comrade, who complimented her on being a Nietzschean supermaid. Sonya swore eternal love for me and I for her; my friend bore solemn witness. She immediately swore sacred and devoted love for my friend, and I was witness in turn. We finally tore ourselves away from Sonya and departed for our cabins.

Sonya went from the boat straight into the arms of a butcher, an American cousin who had imported her as his bride. (Afterward I often saw her staring out of a Harlem butcher shop. She would stand in the window, and between the sections of beef looked like a mournful calf with foolish, large yearning eyes.)

I did not go to the prairies or to the whippoorwill, but actually New York to an uncle, a cigar-maker, who unwilling to lose a day's work, did not even come to meet me.

I felt sick at heart. My entire pose of sophistication suddenly began to disappear in the warm commotion of kisses and embraces, of shouts of joy, of welcome to the new land. My entry was far from a triumphant one.

A Jew with the insignia from the Hachnosos Orchim, the

101

Transients Welfare Bureau, accompanied me all day in search of my uncle, who had changed addresses a number of times since sending me the steamship ticket. It was fortunate that the Jew from the Hachnosos Orchim had patience. Nevertheless, I watched him like a precious gem. I was afraid that at any moment his patience might end and he would lose me, abandon me!

The German's laughter kept haunting me all day, laughter that exploded from a mouthful of large golden teeth: "The Jews are searching for uncle."

Dark elevated trains clattered overhead. Heavy wagons rumbled by. From a store a phonograph ground out the song: "The prayer shawl is still the only consolation."

The tears froze within me. This cold reception put me to sleep like a bear and left me in hibernation for a good many years.

The Bessarabian from Bogota almost kissed me when he spotted me on deck.

"You can't imagine how I've been looking for you! I love you like a brother. And do you know why? Because you have a pair of golden ears. Your ears are worth a million! You can sit and listen and listen. You may really wish me nine ells under, and my words may be going in one ear and out the other, yet you sit and listen. I'm a broken man, and when I get depressed I have to get it off my chest. But go talk if people do not listen! I speak, and see a mouth all set to answer. To speak from one mouth to another is awful! I'm no better. I've got no patience either when someone starts pounding my ear. But when I speak to you, it's to a pair of darling ears. You know, you don't realize what you're worth. If I had such ears, I'd rent them out."

Off in a corner a young girlish voice and two tenors were harmonizing in a Hebrew song.

"Do you know who they are? Hebrew teachers. A young couple and a friend. They had good positions and left them to go to Palestine. You can't imagine how I envy them! Ah, Eretz Yisroel! The patriarchs in the twin caves, Mother Rachel's tomb, the Western Wall! When I think of Eretz Yisroel, little Hebrew letters

102

whirl before my eyes. I remember my *melamed*, a pious Jew with a long, white beard—he himself looked like one of the patriarchs. You remember? Jacob is lying in bed, his twelve sons gathered about him, while he with gaunt neck like my teacher's chants to Joseph: I trouble you thus with my burial, but did not go to such lengths for your mother Rachel. You remember? What a question whether you remember. For me though, it's gone as if through a sieve; just a word remains here and there. But in Eretz Yisroel they speak Hebrew as if they were out of the Bible. . . . Well, excuse me, I must run and change. After all, it's the last night and I have to take a turn on the dance floor. You see, I believe in living, because we all end up the same. But for God's sake, let's see you in the morning before we leave the ship! I must shake your hand and thank you for your golden ears!"

The ballroom was crowded. The dancers were jostling one another. The odor of perspiration was overpowering but the couples floated by elegantly on the closely packed floor. The tall pianist appeared distraught as he tried to push through to the door leading to the bar.

"*Et tu?*" he exclaimed when he saw me. "You also in this Turkish bath with the women?" He seized my hand and deftly maneuvered me and himself out of the ballroom.

The bar was also filled. The pianist found a nook and we seated ourselves. "English breeding" had had a drink too many—the laughter was freer and louder than ever.

The Russian group was at the large center table, with Sonya Yakovlyevna at its head. She was bedecked in a Turkish shawl spread over a garish embroidered dress, and was wearing large, black, pendant earrings.

"*Sonyetchka* you're simply bewitching!"

At another large table youth was having its fling. Three unusually attractive girls of fifteen or sixteen, with painted cheeks and mascara-shadowed eyes, were drinking with five or six young men in tuxedos. The girls wore absurdly long gowns, cut very low, revealing bared backs and the quicksilvery path trembling between their almost completely exposed breasts. The entire group gave the

103

appearance of "playing house" in father's trousers and mother's gowns.

Their chaperone, a woman with a hard, shrewd face and stringy silver-gray hair, was seated near us. She had unearthed a tall, elderly man the very first night, and had become so involved with her own morals, that her three charges freely and openly danced, drank, and disappeared into strange cabins.

The chaperone was tipsy, but not befuddled. Every now and then one of the girls rose, stepped over to kiss her on the forehead and say "Darling!" and returned to the group.

"I have to watch these young bitches," she remarked to her elderly cavalier after taking a sip from her glass, "but you can't tell whether there's anything left worth watching. You ought to see them under the shower! When I look at their straight, glistening bodies and wonderful legs, I say to myself: 'Good night, Mary, time to retire!' "

It became warmer and more crowded. Overheated couples came in from the ballroom. My pianist, who had already emptied several glasses, suddenly glared at me with popping eyes.

"You too hate me!" he screamed. Rising on stiff legs he staggered out of the bar.

Not until I was left alone did I realize that the deck was barely rolling and that this was our last night on the ocean.

"No sleeping tonight. Tonight we'll guide the ship to shore with our own eyes."

It was the Wisconsin schoolmistress. She had managed to locate me.

"Am I disturbing your solitude? You know, the young musicians are here. They're waiting on deck. It's a beautiful night."

Without waiting for my answer, she took my hand and let me out. As we passed the Russians, the blond fellow jumped up.

"*Ni, ni,* that doesn't go tonight! No individualism tonight. Tonight we're all collectivists. No love! No passion! Tonight we're together and we love one another together."

"*V'samum dyelye,*" said Sonya, "do remain with us!"

We excused ourselves and escaped from their friendliness after promising to meet them on deck later.

On one of the companionways leading to the upper deck the teacher stopped. She hesitated for a moment, then buried her head in her hands and burst into sobs. This came so unexpectedly that I began to choke up, and my hands trembled helplessly. In a quavering voice I tried to calm her.

She stopped crying as unexpectedly as she began.

"Forgive me! I'm a big overgrown fool." She wiped the tears from her eyes with her fists, like a little girl. "I warned you I'd do this."

We went up silently. She clung to me and I had the feeling that she had confided something important to me, although I did not know exactly what.

On deck it was cool and spacious. Islets appeared in the water, as if large bites out of the ocean had been replaced with land. The water was smooth and calm now. Our liner was floating like a rowboat and the propeller blades were plashing like oars.

Quivering red and green lights winked at us from afar. Not only did everything appear now just as it had when the ship departed, but there was even the same odor of tar, earth, and shore. Our ship was moving more slowly. It seemed to be taking the leisurely strokes of a confident swimmer.

Conversations were hushed. The tall dark diplomat from Haiti was elegantly promenading his Latvian lady and stooping every now and then to whisper something into her ear and kiss her. The young book publisher was walking arm in arm with a stout wench whose large unprepossessing cat's eyes flashed and glittered in the dark.

The young musicians leaning over the railing were gazing down at the water. Far off somewhere, a narrow patch of light was warming up a strip of water and indicating the spot where the sun would presently emerge.

I felt a sudden languor in all my limbs. Our ship was signaling and several boats answered the echo. I escorted the teacher to the young musicians and begged to be excused.

105

Sleepy seamen were washing down sections of the deck. They barely moved and did not exchange a single word among themselves. The water had wakened musty odors from the wood. The sailors swayed as if asleep. I asked one for the time. Several answered simultaneously, like automatons.

Still a full six hours before landing.

I felt that I must relax on my bunk for a few hours. The corridors were already literally barricaded with piled-up valises and heavy trunks. The dark passageways now appeared even darker. Couples were pushing along the walls and crawling over heaped-up luggage. Three tall youths were supporting, almost carrying, the three slim young girls. Each leaned on her escort with head thrown back. A cabin door opened and they disappeared. The blond Russian was leading the middle-aged Englishwoman. He hurried her along as if afraid that the boat would soon stop. She followed him like a calf, with unwilling steps. She was drunk, belching as she muttered:

"Darling, no one, no one ever did this to me! I have sons almost your age! Where are you taking me?"

The Russian answered: *"Nu da, nu da!"* and continued dragging her to the door. The stewards, perched like Buddhas atop the large trunks, puffed at their pipes and did not even raise an eyebrow.

My neighbor, an elderly schoolmistress of about sixty, was standing near her cabin and fumbling with the key at the lock. When she noticed me, she began to speak as if to herself.

"I'll be in Spain this year. I've gone there for the last thirty years. What's the difference? Is Italy any more interesting? I'm a teacher of Spanish, so I go to Spain. If I were a teacher of German, I'd probably go to Germany. In that case it would be remarkable if I were to go to Spain. Maybe my fate is tied up with Spain."

She yawned, fumbled with the key.

"Good night, *buenas noches,* as they say in Spain."

I lay on the bunk and tried to keep my eyes open, as if afraid of missing something.

106

When I awoke I had a strange sensation. My whole body had suddenly become heavier and had lost the rhythm to which it had become adjusted. I felt a physical change in all my limbs and realized instinctively that the vessel had docked.

VII

Estrangement occurred far more readily than reconciliation. We all stood about with our opened luggage in the large waiting room on the pier, avoiding each other's glances. If our eyes did occasionally meet, we smiled sheepishly as though ashamed of the bacchanalia of camaraderie that had seized us during five whole days.

Everyone had reestablished himself according to his previous sense of decorum, each conscious of the duties and prejudices that had been in a state of suspension for a while. Countenances were as cold and reserved as the faces of the customs officers who were burrowing into valises.

The change in apparel was equally startling. One would never have expected that such a strange hat would sprout atop the crown of red hair seen daily being whipped by the sea breezes. One would never have believed that a new hat or topcoat or a different suit would so alter a visage or the appearance of an individual whom one had observed daily in informal attire. Perhaps the familiarity and companionship of the past few days was due partly to the informality of dress. The interlude which most of us were trying to forget now lay packed away in valises, along with the snapshots and other mementos of the voyage. Now the mechanical fingers of the customs officers were handling and reshuffling them, and the more often these trivialities reappeared,

108

the more indifferent one became to them.

A trace of sociability re-emerged on the Paris-bound train racing through the soot-laden villages and over the fallow fields, after the porter had tossed the baggage through the window into the first available car.

Where were all those pleasure tourists who travel simply to Paris, Italy, England, Ireland, Switzerland, Spain? From where had so many Jews suddenly made their appearance? Aboard ship, they were barely evident; here, they were congregated in the cars as if herded into fourth-class compartments. Their faces were somber. Although the smug, rich uncle was traveling presently to a poor relation, he already began to resemble him slightly. He was recalling, remembering the long ago. The American polish of twenty, thirty, forty years was dissolved from their faces. All are homeward bound, all have suddenly become Rumanian, Polish, Lithuanian. . . .

The other cars were for luxury tourists, but here sat individuals traveling with a purpose, and the sense of obligation lay heavily upon them.

I looked at the gloomy faces and it occurred to me that some twenty-five years later this type of traveler will have disappeared completely. These were the last remnants of an old generation visiting ancestral graves. Nearly all the fathers and grandfathers have already passed away and even the sons are slowly dying off. When the sons' sons visit Russia, Poland, Lithuania, Romania someday, it will be for pleasure only. For them Poland will be like a summer voyage to Paris, Switzerland, Italy. None will be traveling homeward, but merely to get valises plastered with foreign stickers. None will be traveling in search of their origin. That Poland will be dead, as well as the nostalgia or hatred for it. They will be traveling as tourists, not to visit dying or dead parents. In a quarter of a century something will be missing in these cars.

The fields that flitted by were dust-laden and barren-looking.

The grass appeared dusty and parched. From other cars loud laughter could be heard. The tourists were laughing, but here in our ghetto it was already packed with Jewish troubles. But no matter how packed, Jew after Jew kept wandering in.

Where's a Jew going? To Poland. To Rumania. What, to Czechoslovakia? To . . . to . . . to. . . .

When the train arrived at Gare St. Lazare in the afternoon a depressing rain was pouring down, and though it was early July there was a chill in every drop,

The bent figure of the porter resembled a packhorse under the heavy load of luggage on his back. He lumbered along like an elephant, legs spread wide apart.

From the hotel window everything appeared commonplace. Apparently the rain had much to do with it. There is no more ordinary phenomenon than a drenching rain that washes away every distinctive trace of glamour and charm from houses, rooftops, and people.

A side window of the hotel looks down upon a crooked alley running at an incline between brownish houses with peeling walls. A man wearing a beret, with hands thrust in his pockets, was scampering like a cat between the narrow walls. He ran back again. A woman on high crooked heels came hurrying along the narrow sidewalk. It seemed as if at any moment the filthy street would spill her out as from a slop pail. She would surely tumble against the opposite wall and her little traw hat would fly off her head. My heart missed a beat—she was looking up at the window and yawning. She had a mournful, phlegmatic face.

It rained and rained. I lay on the bed and sought a key with which to open the new city, but the rain washed all my thoughts into a jumble.

A woman of about thirty entered. She handed me soap and towels, and filled the bathtub. She came in and left with indifferent steps. As she strode down the corridor, I kept thinking of her unconcern.

The maid returned, shut off the faucet, went out again and

110

slammed the door. I splashed in the bathtub and was thoroughly disappointed.

A large clock was visible from my hotel window. The heavy hand skipped along regularly . . . I must leave in the evening and time is flying. Where shall I start?

I took a taxi and began my round of addresses. Nobody home—out of town. I was alone in a rain-drenched city among soaked monuments and police uniforms.

The Dome was quite empty. Only a few seats were occupied. German, Russian, French, and English newspapers were being read over cups of coffee. An artist who had been to the United States several times sat at one of the small tables. Short and stout, he had a dour oriental face with slanted eyes. I joined him and remarked that I had just arrived from America. It did not make the slightest impression. He stared at me coldly. Nor did he become enthused at the information that I was a writer. Indirectly he tried to determine what sort of writer I was—whether I knew this person, that one.... When I acknowledged knowing the former or the latter, he was still not completely reassured. But he seemed almost convinced that at the worst he would not be taking too great a risk of endangering his reputation because of me.

So he said almost intimately, "I have sad news for you. Bialik is dead."

I was stunned. He pulled out a telegram.

As when a thunderbolt strikes nearby, such is one's reaction each time any one in the profession dies. A crash, a fall—fear and relief that it was someone else.

"A great Jew! What am I saying? The greatest Jew! A great man!"

I was afraid to utter a word lest it fall short of his tone of lamentation.

"The greatest poet since Yehuda Halevi! He surely would have gotten the Nobel prize!"

"He had so much life in him," I dared to inject into his eulogy. "Youthful eyes, a massive head, thick neck, and a laborer's slightly stooped shoulders. He bore a great part of the Jewish burden upon

111

them."

"You knew him?" he exclaimed, and his little Chinese eyes grew even smaller.

"No, but I saw him. Three times."

I awaited his request to impart my meagre reminiscences of the three occasions when I had seen and heard Bialik, but he was still paddling like a plump duck in a reservoir of his own mournful exclamations. He tried to impress upon me that there was a great difference between *my* deceased Bialik and *his*. For me the national poet had died, but every Jew in the street owns a tiny share in the poet. For him, however, since *he* is entirely Eretz Yisroel, is one with the country and spirit, is himself a national poet, and since he had known Bialik intimately—had been an habitue at his home, had seen him presiding at *oneg sabbath* afternoon receptions—for him then his *own* Bialik had passed away. He felt now—he sought a fitting simile—as if his own uncle, who had been a scholarly Jew, had died. True, the whole city lamented because a fine Jew, a great *giver*, a man of dignity had died. Nevertheless it was as if it were his uncle. Did I comprehend?

I was vanquished. I capitulated completely, especially when he told me that he had quite a bit of property in Palestine.

"Real estate, as you Americans call it. I bought it all with art. Art, true art, pays; don't listen to what foolish youths will try to tell you here in Paris."

So I had no alternative but to surrender myself to my poor share in Bialik. I recalled that the first time I saw him was in the midst of great excitement. It was at a banquet arranged by Yiddish writers in his honor. Bialik spoke—rather, chatted in a warm voice. He really wove his speech, like a spider sending out threads in all directions—harmless, gentle threads. Well-phrased sentences.

Everything he said appeared to slip out involuntarily as if he had not meant to utter it. However, in the unintentional there lay a design, as there is a plan in the spun strands of a web. This was not apparent until after he had concluded. During the talk

112

everything seemed pleasant, as if heard in a half doze. But when he had finished speaking, one perceived that all these harmless, scattered threads were one web and that a fly was struggling in it. The fly was—Yiddish.

Yiddish lay there almost strangled. It was recalled that, after all, Bialik had spoken so sweetly about the scores of jargons that the Jews had possessed and which had disappeared. He had really said that one Jew in Eretz Yisroel was worth ten in the Diaspora.

When Bialik finally sat down and we realized that he had given up hope for our life, a storm broke loose. There was something unreal about it. In the clamor Bialik seemed more invulnerable than all of us, but for that very reason did not show any semblance of complacency. We became more aroused more excited, because we did not succeed in raising the counterattack to Bialik's level; however, we appeared more tragic and therefore possibly more righteous.

Among us were idealists, descendants of the eternal Jewish martyrs, and they were immediately ready to agree with Bialik. Their eyes flamed with an insane fire. Their nostrils flared as if already scenting the sacrifice for the Eternal People, for the eternal holy tongue!

There were others, who agreed with Bialik even more energetically—and more sadistically. They sensed the golden opportunity to get rid of their comrades' wealth. They themselves had contributed very little to the last jargon. Then why concern themselves if it were destroyed, consumed? Let the smoke reach the very heavens! Much of what they said had the false ring of counterfeit coins.

The shamed ones appeared truly tragic, as if their tongues had been cut out. They stood facing Bialik, roared like mutes, banged on the table, and I believe balled their fists as well.

I too tagged along with the shamed and insulted ones. My heart was wrung for my few score poems that were to be destroyed here in the conflict over language, and I banged on the table along with the others.

Bialik's cheeks were flushed. He avoided looking into our faces.

113

His forehead glistened. He appeared somewhat inquisitorial when he began to speak again. Perhaps our demand that he give us back our mother tongue pained him, but he bowed his back still further and suffered the burden of our grievances. Nevertheless he had no word of consolation for us. He threatened us with the gruesomeness and inevitability of history as if to say: Little calves, poor creatures, you struggle, you do not wish to be slaughtered, but you will be nevertheless!

Several days later I was sitting with a colleague in a nook of a quiet hotel. Bialik sat between us. My colleague had been sent by his paper for an interview with the great Hebrew poet. It seemed that Bialik distinctly remembered that I had just recently stood screaming at him. He avoided my gaze, as if indebted to me for some article that he could not possibly return. However, after momentary diversions I would often catch him sneaking a glance at me. Invariably he would sigh afterward.

The third and last time, I had seen Bialik on a platform among Hebraists. When he began to speak, a brief conflict broke out. Cries of "Sephardit!" and "Ashkenazit!" were heard. Bialik silenced the clamor by weaving his way between both accents. At this soiree, boys, girls, Hebrew teachers, and several beaming old Jews in skullcaps were present. The latter kept their eyes blissfully shut. What Bialik was saying concerned them little. The important thing was—the holy tongue! The younger folks sat with half-open mouths—after all, Bialik! . . .

Not until I had reviewed these fragmentary reminiscences did I noticed that the artist had left me. He was now seated with a plumpish woman. His profile was toward me and I looked for a trace of his erstwhile grief. Instead, a broad smile was on his wrinkled visage that had the shade of black pepper.

The woman was ugly but I concluded that according to the trite plot formula, she was the symbol of life that had expunged the death of his "personal" national uncle.

I sensed someone's glance To my great surprise, at the next table to the left, the Wisconsin schoolmistress was seated before a half-emptied glass of beer. We looked at each other for a moment

114

as if to determine how much estrangement had taken place since we left the boat, and to what extent we wished to remain estranged. I was so surprised that I even forgot to greet her.

She picked up her glass of beer and joined me at my table.

"What is this, espionage?" she asked. "If I had known that you were one of those fellows who heads straight for the Dome, I wouldn't have spoken a word to you on the ship."

I explained that I was of that vile trade which unites one Dome with another. In our travels we seek out the Dome in every capital. Just when, under such circumstances, we find time to see and speak to real people is a question. Nevertheless, we write books, and people think they are slices of life. In reality they are slices of Dome.

"In that case, let's go somewhere else."

She took me to a small clean restaurant. We sat outside, gazed at each other, and were silent.

"There's something in the Dome that you don't get here," she remarked. "For instance, courage. In the Dome I had more courage. There I could tell you—oh, many things. There's something in its atmosphere. Here I feel conventional once more."

"Why not return?" I half-rose from my chair.

"No! Too late. I'm starved."

She ordered an aperitif.

"You're a Jew, aren't you? I know nothing about Jews."

"What makes you think you ought to know anything special about Jews?"

"Forgive me. You're right."

"No, I'm wrong," I teased her.

After lighting a cigarette she asked indifferently, "How long are you staying in Paris?"

"I leave for Poland at midnight. My mother is ill, very ill. I haven't seen her in twenty years. I owe her every minute. I even thought of flying."

"Give me your Polish address and I'll drop you a line. For you it'll be greetings from the Dome, and maybe from the English language as well, with your folks speaking Polish."

"Yiddish."

"Yiddish! Yiddish! Languages always seem strange to me. The French speak French, the Turks Turkish. Jews speak Yiddish, and Americans will soon be speaking American. Odd but quite natural. They speak their own languages which they themselves have developed. It's as personal as breathing. They don't have to translate, but open their mouths and speak native words: bread, water, butter, milk, cow, grass, sky, heart, sun, star, and love. I hate the other words that make one too smart. Every language should remain naive, simple, and not adopt all the intelligent bastard words that manage to survive in all languages. The grandson ought to speak the identical words of the grandfather."

She took several quick puffs, flipped away the cigarette, and continued:

"I once went to visit my kinfolk, somewhere in a small Swedish village. My parents were born in Wisconsin but my paternal grandfather returned to his birthplace as soon as my father and the other children could stand on their own. My grandfather could never get accustomed to the new country. In the small Swedish village I did not even need an address to locate him. He would pinch my cheeks while his second wife, my step-grandmother, would eye me angrily. She was probably afraid I came for some legacy, and she had several children—I didn't count how many—even younger than myself. Other members of my family: tall, six-foot uncles with thick artificial-looking sidewhiskers, drank to my health, laughed loudly and jabbered, but I didn't understand a word. At night, some strong foolish relative sneaked into my bed. I no longer remember just what the relationship was. He stank of sweat and leather and I quickly decided that it did not pay to struggle with such an idiot. Why shriek and cause a scandal in a small village? Better to give in for a few minutes and get rid of him. However, it seemed that he liked it and on the following day wanted nothing less than to marry me. He even sent my grandfather as matchmaker. My grandfather kept pinching my cheeks and urging the match in whatever broken English he still remembered I left without saying good-bye. . . ."

116

And I too practically ran away from my town, because for me my birthplace had always been fear. A Jewish child grows up on fear. Many of our holidays are panic—the candles are expiring souls. Our funerals are gloomy and our dead live on in their death to terrify the children. Even when dreaming one must keep his wits, so as to remember what to say to a beckoning spectre. In our house, in the cellar, there lived a Jewish baker who helped wash and prepare the dead for the hereafter's final accounting. He washed the dead and kneaded the small rolls that my mother bought each morning. They stuck in my throat more than once; for me they were dead rolls. But our funerals are the epitome of gloom and sorrow. If, in childhood, one has not seen a Jewish funeral in a small village, he does not know what fear really is. Even the dogs whine, for the Angel of Death, as Jewish children know, has a thousand eyes and it would do no good to hide even under the heavy feather quilt. I recall when my mother was ill—she was never well—and I, I don't know whether half-awake or in a dream, pleaded with God that if it were not possible to save her, at least He grant her several more years until I left for America. (Even in my childhood I dreamt of going to America.) I would not have survived a funeral in my home—my mother's funeral—at that time.

Now my mother is very ill. She is calling me home, who knows why. Probably the postponed funeral. I have already traveled two-thirds of the way, wanting to escape my mother's funeral. But go and escape—beat your head against a steel wall! . . . Late. . . . I must go.

"It's getting late. Come, see me to a taxi. I mustn't miss the train."

On the way, again going past the Dome, I met a young artist from New York who had been living in Paris for the last few years and came to New York occasionally to visit relatives.

"You in Paris? At last! It's about time. When did you arrive?"

"Just a while ago and—I'm off again."

"You ought to be ashamed of yourself! Paris and I, we'll never forgive you."

117

"I'll be back."

"In that case. . ."

The Wisconsin schoolteacher looked at us. She had recovered from the rather abrupt intimacy with me. So she stood and gazed coldly at the two of us.

"Who's this *shiksa*?" He looked at her with the frank and almost insolent curiosity that only artists can carry off with suavity.

"Someone from the boat."

"A *shiksa* from the boat and so soon at the Dome? Something's wrong," he said with a singsong inflection.

He suddenly changed from Yiddish to English: "What's doing in New York?"

"I'll answer all your questions when I return. It's almost eleven. I'l miss my train!"

His face clouded, as if he had taken on all my cares. He hailed a taxi and gave the driver the directions how to get to my hotel, somewhere near the Gare St. Lazare. The schoolteacher meanwhile stood several paces off, evidently ill at ease.

"Let me introduce you," I said, quite at a loss, and with one foot already in the taxi.

"You'll miss your train. We'll get acquainted without your help," the artist urged me on.

Before the door slammed shut, the teacher sprang to the taxi, paused an instant, and stammered:

"I—I hope that your mother—that everything'll turn out well!"

She said it tenderly and with great sincerity. She, from Wisconsin, was sending a gentle greeting to a little village in Poland. It was absolutely the warmest thing she could have said.

She remained standing with downcast eyes, and in them, even more than on her lips, was an unexpressed thought.

With the taxi banging left and right, barely missing a score of people, I wondered whether there would be any harm in turning back and staying for a day or two.

Even while waiting on the station, I still felt some regret.

118

After the ship everything seemed to me like a direct route homeward. I definitely felt that a roomful of troubles awaited me, nevertheless I yearned to get there as soon as possible. Was it a feeling of getting something over with? I hardly think so. I was homesick. I saw myself in various poses at the homecoming: in the droshke, at the door. However I did not dare cross the threshold. I did not wish to spoil that sensation even by dreaming about it. I postponed it for the proper moment.

I was nervous and impatient. I knew that they were just before the last act there in the old house, and were waiting for me to raise the curtain. This act was inevitable, but the entire household was waiting because they did not wish to end the play without me I knew quite well how it would end, and yet was drawn there by the fear that I might miss some of what was destined for those near and dear to me. Who knew whether they would hold out until my arrival?

If on board ship I strolled about as though the deck were a long sunny valley leading nowhere, if my recollections at that time were cold and distant, I now became tense, so that I did not even wish to see anyone. Everything seemed to me an obstacle to the main goal. I no longer cared to involve myself in a strange world with strangers and forced conversations. All this seemed to me now a waste of time. I decided to keep to myself as much as possible. I imagined that I was approaching an eye-opening event that would make clear for me many obscure matters, although I did not know exactly how. Therefore I did not wish to let myself be diverted. It appeared to me that only now was I on the right path and I dared not get lost. The rhythmic beat of the wheels calmed me a little, particularly because the train seemed to be infected with my restlessness. It was running, running, running without pause to my mother. As I sat with eyes shut, it seemed to me that this was the same train that had taken me away from home one midnight twenty years ago. Now too it was past midnight, and a bit of compensation it would be, if this were by some miracle the same train. But when I opened my eyes, the car did not in the least resemble the one of twenty years ago, which I would have recognized even if it were dismantled.

I shut my eyes, though I had no desire for sleep. . . .

A cold shudder awoke me, startling me from my torpor.

I forcibly aroused my sleep-weighted arms and legs, and as if treading on sand with rubber soles that have neither blood nor life in them, managed to drag myself to the narrow corridor.

Dew-moist fields, small towns, and rocky hills raced by the windows. The sky was clouded with a forecast of rain.

Near me stood a short, broad-shouldered man in his early forties, gazing at the fleeting fields, woods, and hamlets. He kept turning toward me as if about to say something, but after each glance fixed his gaze once more on the mist-filmed pane of the car window.

Finally he addressed me in German, and when my reply did not come promptly, he inquired in a broken and hesitant English whether I was an American.

His suit was immaculate, the trousers carefully pressed. Such neatness was remarkable so early in the morning when everyone was just beginning to uncurl from his huddled posture. He was not blond with the brazen German blondness—that would not suit his modest bearing. His hair was dark blond, and already salt-and-peppered with steely gray in places. He had a large face with somewhat near-sighted, sad eyes.

He was a manufacturer returning home from Paris. He once did considerable business with America. "But now," he laughed as if it were some kind of joke, "America has stopped trading with us. Canada, on the other hand, is still a good buyer."

"America is boycotting?" I asked with as much indifference as possible.

He laughed as though he were greatly pleased, as though the entire matter were child's play and he an adult spectator.

"Yes. . ."

"How are things?" I continued very discreetly, seeking to gain his confidence.

"Not very good. The workers are very destitute; many factories are vacant." His silk factory too, he told me candidly, had to dismiss half its employees.

120

"How will it all end?' I asked, more boldly.

He glanced at me and began to laugh with his myopic-melancholy eyes. He laughed and almost choked with helplessness.

"We mustn't talk, we mustn't say anything! Nothing! It's better so, to say nothing!"

He explained that it was not in his nature to be discourteous to me. His laughter turned into a squeal that was slightly hysterical, like the laughter of some at hearing sad tidings. He even tried to belittle what he had let slip previously, that the factories were empty and the workmen in dire poverty.

"Things will probably improve," he said.

The cars began to awaken and the corridor became noisy. People in dressing robes were passing to and fro. Impatiently they awaited their turn at the washrooms, in which the "bandit" occupants were seated as though in their father's vineyards.

In the morning light the German's face became even more familiar and likable. The brownish eyes were ever ready to smile. His exceptionally broad shoulders possessed great strength, but the face, despite its heaviness and broad features, showed refinement.

Men and their wives were shouting at each other in a New York Yiddish-English, and the German remarked almost respectfully:

"Many Americans are traveling to Europe nowadays."

"Yes, it seems so."

A tall Jew in a bathrobe passed me. He looked sharply into my eyes.

"Y' forgot yer razor!" a woman called after him.

"Dat's right!" He went back, passed me, and again stared sharply into my eyes.

"Vat's amara vit yer towel?" the woman's voice yelled after him again.

"Demmit!" He returned once more, took his towel, passed me, and after a searching glance finally ventured a "Good morning," in a tone he might have used for "*Sholem aleichem,* fellow Jew!"

"Good morning!"

"Good morning!"

Mining villages, sooty houses, work-bound people with small lunch pails floated by. Machinery on rust-stained ground. . . . The train sped onward. The German gazed out of the window, talking as if to himself about Belgium's coal, iron, copper, and zinc mines and its wool, cloth, and silk industries.

The conductor with the well-combed and waxed black little mustache, after passing several times, stopped and beckoned to us. We followed him as he led us mysteriously into a separate car. He opened the window and told us to look out.

The train was rushing by immense mountain peaks which had no perceptible slope, immense vertical walls that darkened the car as would the longest of tunnels. We looked out and saw nothing, but the conductor's face was full of anticipation. Suddenly he exclaimed:

"Le roi!"

Both of us thrust out our heads. The conductor looked out through another little window. We twisted our heads upward but could not see to the top of the frightful precipice. The train was running more slowly along this gigantic wall which seemed to have all the hues of rusted ore.

Suddenly we noticed flowers at the base of a cliff section, and on its face the date: February 7, 1934, as well as several other words which we failed to grasp as the train moved on. I realized immediately, however, that on this crag King Albert's career as mountain climber had come to an end. Hard to understand what he could have been seeking in this perilous out-of-the-way place, unless it were death.

The conductor was still looking back at the mountain monument. I craned my neck, and was horrified by the thought that here only a few months ago King Albert had fallen to his death on the spot now marked by the flowers. The conductor drew in his head and sat exhausted, as if he had lived through a trying experience, as if he had been present during King Albert's last moments. He considers us fortunate individuals for having had the privilege of seeing what no one else in the train had seen. When we thanked him for his thoughtfulness he acknowledged it

122

with a grimace, implying that nothing we possessed could adequately pay for the thrilling moment he had vouchsafed us.

I got out at the station. Small trucks loaded with baggage were being pulled joltingly over the cobblestones. Conductors were seated on the car steps, basking in the sun. Small groups stood about chatting. I looked for a Jewish face.

A stately, attractive young girl with serious eyes that appeared almost angry and unfriendly was pacing back and forth. She looked to be about sixteen or seventeen, but there was a world of sorrow in her countenance. She walked with head held high and proudly, a rare mixture of youthfulness and earnestness. Impossible to gaze at her with the lascivious stare used to appraise young girls. Staring back with stern eyes as if she were twisting your ears for your effrontery, she appeared older in wisdom than you. You knew that it would be a great achievement to kindle even a tiny flame of happiness in such intelligent, somber eyes. A tall, elderly woman in black approached and took the young girl by the arm. Both strolled up and down silently. Were they Jewish?

The German was also walking to and fro on the platform. He now seemed much shorter than before, as if shrunken. He was somewhat ashamed to look me directly in the face, so walked behind me like a shadow. He passed by several times and gazed at me with the eyes of an unfortunate cow. He wished to determine if we were still on speaking terms. He shrugged his shoulders, gestured with his hand in helplessness, wrinkled his brow, as if to say: what can one man do?

When the train started we were seated together at a small table in the diner. The train lurched. A fat, uniformed German was serving food from a large metal platter. He did not look like a man at all; moved about like a massive woman, and even his wrinkled face resembled that of an old faithful cook. When everyone had been served, he added an extra portion to each plate with womanly tenderness.

The German and I sat opposite each other. He ordered a bottle of wine and poured a glass for me too. I did not touch it.

123

It looked like a homey private restaurant. There was something village-like in the food, in the service, and in the fat old German waiting on us.

My table companion urged: "Do drink something! Do eat something!" As if in answer to my thoughts he carried on a conversation of asides about the permanent aspects of life which do not change, which will always endure; about the friendly atmosphere in the dining car; about human kindness which will triumph—all else are sad events which will vanish. "Do drink! Do eat!" But I found it difficult to do so—as if someone were gently choking me, not yet constricting but holding my throat and ready to strangle.

I felt the same way later when my German alighted and bade me a warm farewell, assuring me again that everything would yet be set aright. I wished to ask him how, since all were meanwhile obediently raising their hands aloft, but I took pity on him. He kept shouting back to me, *"Danke schoen! Danke schoen!"*

That is how I felt all day while the train panted across German soil. The few Jews in the car, who were playing cards and not even glancing out of the window, felt the same way. Berlin aroused a little interest. We got off and trod cautiously, as though having no right of residence there, as if we were present illegally. . . .

Toward evening the rich, fertilized fields vanished. Lean, faded patches of ground appeared with less green in the verdure, less richness in the black soil, and less orderliness. Everything was helter-skelter. Here the seeds had landed and something was growing; there they had not fallen—a patch of grass was flourishing.

Two small deer stood gazing at the train. They were glued to the spot and paralyzed with fear. Only when the train had passed did they leap away with marvelous grace, hopping on their forelegs, hind legs appearing to hang in midair.

Night was already blackening the windows completely, and when several narrow-shouldered conductors appeared and I heard the first Polish words, my heart became lighter. The clutching

124

hand around the throat was gone, and the comical, utterly strange train conductors who looked like dressed-up Sabbath-*goyim*, became as close as one's own townsfolk.

Incomprehensible! . . .

Apparently I had put myself at God's mercy, because when I opened my eyes I heard someone shouting:

"Zgersz! Zgersz!"

My sleepy head got me to my torpid feet. Zgersz meant my brother Benjamin, my brother Marcus.

Zgersz—Marcus, Benjamin!

I hurried to the window. Maybe I would see familiar faces.

The train did not even stop. I dropped back on the bench and was completely erased under the rubber wheels of a dream which rode over my crushed bones. It was a deep phantasmagoria, deep as a well, and I lay at the very bottom, drowned. I was certain that I would save myself, but did not know when. . . . It must have been quite a number of hours before I forced my eyes open.

Tumbledown huts . . . peasants escorting the train with sleepy, sad eyes. Barefoot peasant women standing like Madonnas with infants in their arms, as if holding them before our eyes and pleading: "Here, at least take the children from us; make our burden lighter!" The children lay motionless, with the same sad eyes as the old peasants—supplicating eyes. The wheels sped even faster.The eyes pursued us: *Bread!* The fleeting wheels as if a curse were on them went on clicking. Bread! Bread! Bread!. . . Hard to forget such eyes. . . .

Black chimneys, smoke, soot, and an unbelievable word:

Warsaw.

The coachman yanked at the reins and the lean, spare horse jogged off with the jiggling droshke. The Warsaw streets still lay half asleep. It was hot, unusually hot for a morning. The fatigue of a day and a half on the train curled me up alongside my luggage. The streets unwound themselves and rolled up with a remarkable strangeness. My head felt heavy and I kept pulling it back as it sank forward. It was as if for a score of years I had

125

worn myself out waiting for this very moment, and now that it had come I was too tired to extend a welcoming hand.

My head was filled with an old jumble of the last few drowsy and rackety early-morning hours on Polish soil. My brain was now reviving identical dreams as occur sometimes when one awakens, dozes off again, and continues dreaming the same thing with a sleepy consciousness.

This time, however, I was not continuing but actually repeating a dream. I strove to restore in it the same lightness and illogic. Nevertheless my brain was now more alert, and things fell into an undesirable order willy-nilly. The fragments of dream had the appearance of design.

Too much translation from hieroglyphics into intelligible language was going on within me. Everything that had been lazy and formless while I lay at the very depth of the dream now assumed dimensions and limits. The first dream was a live anthill, but in the redreaming I had stirred up the hill, and episodes—separately recognizable episodes—begin to scurry into warmer corners.

The background of the dream was a vague sort of fear of an Angel of Death. Deep-toned Russian and Polish church bells were pealing, and someone with a crooked stick like a branch was hurrying downhill along the Jews' street, knocking at all the shops, warning of the approach of the Sabbath eve. Shops closed in sleepy obedience. An awesome calm fell upon the barred shops and shadowed, empty streets.

In the midst of the massive Greek Orthodox churches and the slenderer Catholic ones stood the tumbledown house of study, the *bethmedrash*. The street leading to the sacred place was dark, and from the *bethmedrash* joyous cries of welcome to the Sabbath burst forth.

A tall water-carrier was walking with slow ponderous strides alongside a small Jew. To me it was clear that this small Jew was the rabbi Reb Eisener Kopp, but he gazed up at the tall one with great awe.

"Rebbe," he said to the water-carrier, "you do know how to

stop oppression. Will you, Rebbe, permit this punishment—that the destroyer should make desolate the entire sacred community?"

"Don't call me Rebbe," the tall water-carrier, who during the day was a timid creature with drooping shoulders, exploded into violent anger. "Don't try to put the rebbe's fur cap on my head! I don't consent! I'll not allow it!"

The small, gentle Jew who had until now been walking calmly also became bitterly enraged. He clipped his words so that his voice seemed to come out muffled.

"If you're going to play the humble and simple creature, we'll be left as sheep without a shepherd. There is no one from whom to take counsel. The Angel of Death is almost at the gates of the city and you dilly-dally with humility!"

Beresh's shoulders sagged as if he were carrying the heaviest load of the day. He bent double and leaned against the smoking lamppost while sobbing silently.

From the *shul* sprightly *l'cho dodi's* kept resounding through the dark street. The bells swung devoutly over the entire city and the Lublin town clock struck midnight.

Then two pairs of heavy boots came striding up the muddy road. When they reached the other side of the cemetery, which was beyond the town's environs, they paused. A sickly sun gave the mist-laden sky the semblance of day. Both pairs of boots, certain now that they were treading on city ground, were permitting themselves the pleasure of a slight rest.

The tall Jew with the flaming red beard and small green eyes groaned deeply and began to scrape his torn cotton cloak intently. The short Jew beside him barely came up to his belt. He had a gray, thatchy beard and red cheeks like frozen apples. He did not let go of the tall one's hand, though the latter struggled to free himself. The tall one snarled and the little Jew pinched his hand sharply, playfully, producing such a bellow that his nose began to run. And no sooner did I hear his bellow than I recognized him immediately as the crazy Abish.

It was not quite daylight. Nevertheless, little barefooted urchins were stamping about in the mud puddles. As soon as they noticed

127

the two leaning against the barrier, they exclaimed: "The crazy Abish is here, the crazy Abish!" The gleeful shouts echoed over the length of the new road . . . .

A gentle lad with demure cheeks was going to *cheder*. He had a fresh *pletzl* spread with melted butter, a bag of sour cherries, and in his pocket a two-kopek piece for ice cream. The boy was so very familiar that I almost cried. He stopped and then boldly approached Abish, pinched out a piece of *pletzl*, and extended his hand. But when Abish tried to grab it, the lad merely hinted in a quiet voice: *Vechol ma-aminim.*

Abish's green eyes lit up. Dutifully and piously he swayed back and forth, and with drawn lips sang each verse with proper stress and emphasis:

> *Vechol ma-aminim*
> It's God one must serve—
> Him one must serve.
> Him one should serve
> With joy and delight—
> Who ransoms from death and the pit.

The small Jew, his father, swayed in unison. In his head were born little thoughts of consolation: His son was earning a living, no evil eye befall him! Years and years he has been splashing about with his son in the mire of every town and hamlet, and God is a father! Abish has a talent for singing. They manage to get through the week, blessed be His Name, and every Friday return to hear the Sabbath greeting sung in the Rebbe's hall of study. The father too can sing a *vechol ma-aminim* but not with the son's practiced skill. Parts of his brain are already dulled—the words come out slurred and not as melodious nor with Abish's ease. Without Abish he undoubtedly would have gone under in his old age.

The little boy with the demure cheeks looked around to see whether anyone was observing and handed Abish another pinch of *pletzl*.

"Abish, tell me the time."

The father shut his eyes. He knew what came next. Indeed, he did not approve, but understood that it was part of the job. Abish busied himself at his crotch and took the thing out and clumsily twisted it as though he were winding a clock. The little boy, who had already seen this countless times, uttered a shriek and a giggle, and like a colt galloped off to *cheder*.

At the gentile market place many wagon teams had already driven up—the peasant women with hens and eggs, vegetables and fruit, black and red berries. The housewives blow on the hens at the proper spot and haggle. A peasant stands near his wagon and makes a wide puddle that flows foaming toward the horse, which lifts its hoof. The butchers in bloodied aprons sharpen their long pointed knives. One butcher seizes a young *shiksa*, lifts her into the air, and holds here there. Several of his fellows hurry forward and shove their hands under her dress, which billows in the breeze. The *shiksa* struggles and kicks at them, shrieking, "Of God, of God they aren't afraid, of God!"

The market place smells of mealy, sour peaches, cranberries, raspberries, fresh carrots, lettuce, green-yellow cucumbers, and red radishes, all of which seem to rise before the eyes and fill the entire market place with its aroma.

An old peasant woman, who looks like a witch, milks a submissive goat and hands a freshly filled glassful to a young *chassid* with curled earlocks. After each gulp be puts his hand to his heart, then sips absorbedly as though taking some fine medicine.

In addition to vegetables and fruits, the market smells of cows, hens, and dogs and of horses and their fresh droppings. Angry dogs with old faces are tied to the wagons. They tug at their leashes and bark. Half smothered cocks skillfully extricate their heads from beneath heaps of rags, crow chokingly, and subside into a coma.

A gypsy woman goes about jingling her chains and bracelets and pulling at everyone's sleeve. Jewish women exchange counsel. Jews too are sniffing about, looking for bargains for the Sabbath. Nobody pays any attention to the demented Deborah who pulls

129

up her dress as far as her eyes and shrieks hysterically in her childish lisp: "Jewth, the Methiah will come!"

The day is humid and the peasants perspire in their heavy linen blouses. Slowly their wagons start back for the hamlets, where a cool sky hangs over the huts scattered in the thick woods.

A blind old man sits in the center of the market place, playing on his concertina and singing a devout song which everyone knows by heart. In his hands the concertina seems like a hand organ that keeps grinding out the same tune again and again:

> I am blind,
> But Jesus is good to me—
> Good to me,
> And Maria is good to me—
> Good to me.
> So, dear people, be good to me
> Good to me.

Ripei, ripei, ripei. He extends the bellows of the concertina, which curls in on itself, stretches and twists like a serpent.

The old fellow's singing is cloyingly sweet—but distasteful to all. He is avoided by every one—dogs and horses move aside, and even ducks and hens go around rather than touch him with wing or foot.

An emaciated priest with long thin nose and freckled face pauses near the old man and begins to converse with him in song:

> Good day to you, grandpa,
> Good day unto you.
> How does the Light of your Heart
> Treat you today?

The old chap slowly silences his concertina. He answers with the identical words of his tune, but does not sing. He merely accompanies each few words with a quiet *ripei:*

> Jesus is good to me—

Good to me,
And Maria is good to me.

"That's good!" The black-robed priest piously turns his eyes
skyward. He takes out a groschen, carefully examines it on either
side, and satisfied that the bright little coin is not a goldpiece,
toses it into the beggar's cup. The old fellow immediately begins
to play his little tune and sways his half-bent body.

The priest goes from one stall to the next, where hang rosaries,
copper Jesuses, red icon-lamps, brilliantly painted Marias in gilt
frames, bleeding hearts, and Jesuses with thorns about their blond
heads. He devoutly touches the sacred objects. Women pass by and
devoutly kiss his hand.

He goes over to a young *shiksa* seated among large earthen pots
filled with raspberries. The *shiksa* quickly jumps up, blushes, seizes
his hand and presses it to her lips. The priest takes several berries,
breaks open their delicate, hairy orifices, tosses them into his
mouth, and smacks his lips in satisfaction.

Several he holds in his palm. He looks at the raspberries, which
stand like tiny vases.

"A good crop, a successful crop," the priest mumbles, chewing
the while. "The Lord God has blessed our trees and our earth this
year."

While the priest stands gazing at his palm, which appears blood
stained from the raspberries, the market place suddenly becomes
somber from one end to the other—perhaps because it has become
empty and gloomy with the darkness of a Sabbath eve.

The man with the crooked stick still hurries downhill through
the Jews' street, rapping on all the shops. The priest signals with
his red palm and the deep toned Russian, as well as the Polish
church bells begin to peal. Then they cease, and, since the red
palm does not plead with them, stay silent. The blind beggar
remains seated near an old urine-stained wall on the square and
tugs at the concertina.

I am blind
But Jesus is good to me—

Good to me.
And Maria is good to me—
Good to me.
So, dear people, be good to me,
Good to me....

On the train I had awakened with the flavor of the old fellow's unsavory tune on my palate. Even now as I was being bounced about in the *droshke* I had the same sour taste in my mouth as I had after climbing out of my dreams to discern with sleepy eyes the actual Polish towns and villages flying by the train windows.

I was grateful to my drowsy brain for having woven together this rare hodge-podge. After twenty years I was returning home overladen with hominess and even the sad tonality of home. I now felt as if all my pockets were filled to overflowing with the close-to-home things of my dream over which I had stood guard during the twenty years. I now felt like emptying my pockets and scattering all my recollections over the Warsaw streets. "See, I did not betray your trust! Tongue is indeed stuck to the roof of my mouth now, but I never forgot you, Jewish Poland, with all your fears and tearful merrymaking!

Warsaw in the early morning had not yet greeted me. The peculiar spirit of the city still lay asleep.

This journey of mine to my aunt by way of New York created in me an impression of having gone far out of my way, of having entered through another gate or of having arrived by a back door. Once I was wont to ride directly from Lublin to Warsaw. Now I happened to be riding from Lublin to Warsaw via New York, after a twenty-year almost endless journey.

Languor weighed down every bone in my body. I gazed at the Warsaw streets as through a window, and in the retrospect of years tried to recognize them. A drowsy order reigned over the streets. The droshke was crossing the bridge to Praga. Despite the twenty years of world upheaval my aunt still lived in the same courtyard.

Nevertheless she had experienced a slight change. Whereas she once lived on the right, she now lived on the left. After all, twenty years have gone by!

Though I wished to slip by quietly and unobtrusively, I was

132

unsuccessful. A small girl started running; two little boys grabbed each other's hand and galloped across the yard like couriers. A woman with an oversized nose like a potato wanted to know whom I was seeking. A Jew with a bound-up beard began to shout across the court. Several women appeared on balconies. The entire courtyard came alive.

When I reached the stairs, my aunt was already halfway down and greeted me with a clap of her hands and a distorted face.

Yellow as my aunt's face was, nevertheless it was the only bright spot on the dark stairway. I recognized her immediately.

My aunt led me into the house with a burst of sobbing.

"Your mother is truly a pious creature to have lived to see this day! Your mother must have great merit somewhere in heaven, to have lived to see you!"

For a moment I thought that she had led me into a wax museum. Several figures were standing and observing me.

"Don't you remember them? They're my daughters. This is the youngest one, named after Grandma Dresl . . .You don't remember the middle one either? And you've forgotten the eldest?"

Never until now, while gazing upon the three yellow faces, did I think of the past twenty years in terms of war, hunger, pogrom, fear, poverty, want. Never until now, as I stood rooted to the spot, gazing at the three faces, did I have occasion to think of the twenty awful years as even in the ordinary sense a period of time . . . I had caught them in the act of becoming prematurely old.

One was suffering from goiter; here eyes were balls of glass. Almost all the teeth of the second were gone, and her haunch was triple the breadth of her waist. The third, the youngest, actually had the oldest-looking and most worried face.

Two young men came out of an anteroom. One was introduced to me as the husband of the eldest daughter. He had a sullen and secretive face. He left immediately. He was an unemployed baker and had to hurry to a union meeting.

The other man was my aunt's son, born two years after my departure. Despite his eighteen years, he already had a shining bald

133

pate and the face of a weary merchant.

In the kitchen I changed into some fresh clothing, and washed up at the rusted pump. Meat was soaking on the window sill, and around the meat crawled roaches. These too I had not seen in two decades. Now they pricked my heart no less than they used to prick me as a child when I would step on them with bare feet. The floor, the walls, and the ceiling were literally of the same hue—the color of poverty: not really black, but the muddy black, earth color of things about to disintegrate.

When I re-entered the adjoining room my uncle too was seated there, sipping a glass of tea. Once he had the great black beard of the stout municipal official. Now it had become a small gray beard, not the result of trimming but of shedding. He extended an aged hand in greeting. It was impossible to recognize in him any sign of the vigorous meat dealer of yore whose face radiated such strength that he always appeared to be on the verge of a stroke.

"Set the table! He must be hungry!" my uncle commanded in an aside, not quite certain whether he might still speak to me familiarly. However, despite my frightful hunger, I prudently drank a glass of tea, while thinking of the crawling roaches and the pauperish filth.

A man six feet tall or a mite more entered with a leonine head and a belly like a kettledrum that had split open a way through the widest of trousers. He immediately ran over to me and thrust out a large hand.

"*Sholem aleichem, sholem!* Mother-in-law, is it he?" he wished to be sure.

I was truly grateful to him for bringing a different atmosphere into the home.

"Why so silent here, as if at a funeral? Imagine, a man has just come to Poland and he is immediately handed worries. What's the matter, won't there be time later?"

That big belly of his possessed a mass of energy. Such massive agility I had never seen. He did not remain still for a moment, and flitted about from one to the other with the nimbleness of a dancer.

134

He kissed his mother-in-law, kissed his wife, and told me in one breath that I was invited to his home for lunch. He tore out like a whirlwind, to make the purchases and get things ready.

When his wife has also gone, my aunt began to tell me his enteire "history."

"You see that fat fellow, he's stuffed with knowledge. He himself is to blame for the boor in him. What wasn't poured into him! Courses, the violin, dancing. Gold and silver and jewels, but he never wanted to amount to anything. First of all he fell head over heels in love with my daughter and took her without a stitch. He was pursued with a twenty-thousand dollar dowry—as a groschen buys a begel! He has a profitable trade; he's a dental mechanic. But he hates to work. He has already spent six or seven years in Uruguay. It's only a year since he's back, and he's again packing to be off. He would be a pretty fine chap, but he loves food and drink and, would that it weren't so, even loves to cast an eye on strange young women. He desires everything. He has hungry eyes, a large belly, and a gluttonish throat, but just talk to him. He's really a bit insane, but when he starts talking there's something worth hearing."

At his home he catered to my every comfort. We drank colorless Polish whisky and he simply stuffed me.

"Why do you eat so little, like a bird?" He immediately began to address me in the familiar second-person singular. "Strength lies in the plate. You'll need a good bit of strength coming home to a sick mother."

The more he ate and drank, the more talkative he became.

"As you see me alive, I become wiser with every passing day. I become wiser because I've finally discovered the secret that the more foolish you are, the better. Once I was a complex young man with problems by the bushel. I was continually ailing. Those were the days when I loved nothing but chamber music. You know, intimate, quiet musical conversations."

He sipped another glassful.

"However, I began to reduce backward, and the more I reduced, the larger my paunch grew. I realized that the whole thing was

135

nothing more than imaginary greatness. What's the matter with opera—a bit of Verdi, Bizet, Halevy? And when I got back to opera, I felt that even opera was too highflown for the likes of me. I went way back to the simple melody. A hearty Jewish folktune is just as good. When I had achieved the folksong I first felt revived, as you sometimes refresh yourself with a really sour pickle or tasty sauerkraut.

"Chamber music, that's invalidism, fit for the idle rich, but *volkslied* means to devour, to guzzle, to live. You don't know what living means. The world babbles about heroism, and the heroism in the last analysis means death. It teaches the love of death. What sort of pretense about heroism! If I knew that I was about to die, I'd immediately drop to the floor and bellow so that I'd bring heaven and earth together. For whom must I play the hero here? They all can go to hell. A person is about to leave this earth—is that a matter of no importance? I'd bellow in fear of death because a life, a belly, a mouth was being cut down, eyes were being closed forever. They can all go to hell with their bravery!"

When he had brought me to the station and I was seated on the train to Lublin, he fell on me with his heavy head and kissed me. He still kept affirming that one must return to the simplest *volkslied* and to life.

"Swallow chunks of life! Gobble up, guzzle down as much as possible, and be less of a hero!"

"However," he whispered confidentially, coming as close as his belly allowed, "if you live in Poland and see the worry-laden Jewish faces, you lose your appetite for life. That's why I'm returning to Montevideo soon. The South American Spaniard still knows how to live, and he still allows you to live. 'Live and let live!' Don't mind my using that worn proverb, as long as it means live."

He squeezed my hand warmly, sprang from the moving train and with belly protruding, followed quite a way, waving a handkerchief energetically.

136

A young man of some twenty-odd years entered my compartment. He bowed and sat down opposite me at the window, which kept focusing at bits of forest, field, stream, and summer sky of dull blue, An indifferent sky—it was clear at once that there would be neither lightning, thunder, nor rain all that wearisome day.

The slender young man smiled amiably even before making up his mind to chat.

I asked him to pardon my rusty Polish, explaining that it was the first time in twenty years that I had need to recall it.

"Where from? A stranger?"

"No, but an expatriate. From New York."

"In that case you must put the receivers to your ears and be greeted by our music first of all."

He pointed to the radio earphones and I obediently put them on.

The train sped onward, and with it the squeak of trashy cafe tunes which grated on my ears. However, I was thankful to him for his suggestion. The common Polish songs and their insame words had an inherent charm, were no less different than the Polish panorama—the grass, groves, and valleys which were fleeting by.

"Magnificent," I exclaimed, "the tonal flora and fauna of the land."

"That indeed," said he beaming, "Our poverty, our joy, and our sorrow. Our own."

He began to polish his spectacles and peered at me with lackluster light-brown eyes. Without the glasses they appeared sullen, but were made radiant by a smile. Twenty years ago I had seen few such faces among the youth of Poland. It was a far cry from the flaxenhaired peasant lad with foolish eyes and pimply face to this European visage opposite me. This refined face had been raised in the atmosphere of a fatherland.

I conveyed all this to him in careful phrases, even the comparison to the peasant lad of the past. I assured him that I was as thankful for his musical welcome as for his aspect. It was

137

new and different!

His brow became furrowed and I sensed his anxiety. This young man, I mused had an almost Jewish hump on his back; ours was born of Jewish exile, his under the burden of a young land, a young government with all the ills and afflictions of infancy. He was wearing the yoke of responsible citizenship.

"We are working hard to raise Poland's prestige in the world." He again removed his eyeglasses and began wiping them, but this time in order to avoid my gaze. "You're a Jew, aren't you?" He said *zhid*, but it was spoken softly, without any venom. "There are some among us who drag the fine traditions of Poland to the ground. That's an excrescence. We shall cut it out."

He offered me a firm hand, as if solemnly taking a sacred vow. We understood each other and discussed it no further.

He was a civil engineer. He worked in Warsaw for a while and was now being transferred to another town nearer home.

But he would rather not talk about himself. He bombarded me with questions about America, Roosevelt, and my journey home after twenty years.

He too was homeward bound, but how compare that trip with my pilgrimage! He visited his parents but half a year ago; in my case it was a score of years. Twenty years! He could not cease marveling.

"I should be silent and not disturb your thoughts at this sacred moment. Twenty years of separation from flesh and blood, and now the homecoming! It is a great drama."

I begged him to continue. I told him that after the eight- or nine-day journey across sea and land, I was traveling home alone. It was heartrending. I felt abandoned and forlorn. Only a while ago I had known so many people, and now—all gone, never to be seen again, not even in a score of years. To them I can never return.

"The frivolous, superficial individual," I added, "has a good time. He is a pirate of moments, takes hold of things with good-natured abandon. He takes root nowhere."

I explained further that during the trip I had met some very fine people. I had become accustomed to the flutter of their

138

conversation. Nothing eventual had occurred; they had merely talked, but to me that conversation had been far more intriguing than the most exciting of events.

"Interesting, even when I could hear nothing. About me would be the busy hum of a life of words only, and I would retire to my archives of introspection. Not the action, but the dialogue makes a play—the inflection, the voice, the facial expression. It is my own fault perhaps, somewhat too egocentric of me, yet quite often it would seem as if they were all escorting me homeward. Now they have left me and I am a solitary traveler."

He did not answer immediately and I had time to recall their faces.

"Yes," he said finally, "every individual is an entity of loneliness. However, there are some lonely people who can spread the gaiety and commotion of a jazz band, and others who cannot. But it would be odd," he added smilingly, "if you were to come marching home, after twenty years, with the entire group with whom you had struck up acquaintance during the trip. All must part when it comes to pacing one's *via dolorosa.*"

His mother, he said, could not bear his failure to visit her at least twice a year. He was the apple of her eye, the sole survivor of six children. Two died before he was born, and three had been younger than he. Children are the most uncertain of things in the small Polish hamlet. Until the age of ten or twelve, they cannot, with certainty, be considered members of the family.

"Three of my brothers died. Two before I was born, and I myself saw one little fellow of three or four close his eyes forever."

I turned my head to the window and went off alone—as he had just expressed it, on my *via dolorosa* . . . .Herzke, my little brother, who brought death into our household . . . .Father and several men standing about his cradle as he breathed his last . . . .My father crying with all his might, "Hear O Israel, the Lord our God . . ." Herzke's eyes start, roll upward, and my father escorts his soul with mournful cries of "Hear O Israel" until all is quiet in the cradle . . . .

It was already late in the evening. We had all gone to bed. My

139

father remained alone in vigil over the cradle. Herzke still seemed to be with us that night, still seemed to be one of us. I kept waking as from a delirium, to hear my father murmuring verses of the Psalms and sobbing quietly so as not to awaken anyone . . . .

Early in the morning I was awakened by a sing-song lament, but this time it was my mother's. She sat beside the covered cradle and wailed as if she were reading the Bible in vernacular. Her words were archaic ones, not in common use, taken from sacred books. Her devout Jewish patience was quite gone. She was carrying on a dispute with God. She was making accusations.

I wandered about the house a bundle of grief. I ached all over. It hurt me even to breathe. I tortured myself not to breath and when I could no longer bear it, would catch my breath in groans. I begged my mother to at least let me kiss his blond head, but she brokenly explained to me that it was against the Jewish ritual. Neverthless she had to yield to me and uncover his countenance.

"You see now, my child, what has become of his angelic face!"

I was overcome with grief. My mother still was belaboring God with arguments. She was aiming her arguments at the ceiling, directly to Him, and demanding justice of Him. "Is it right that so young a joy be cut down and sent to an early grave? Why did so innocent a soul deserve an untimely death?"

There came no answer from the ceiling. I felt that she had not sufficiently shaken the Throne of Glory to its foundations. I recalled that two of my brothers had died before I was born. Now I came to my mother's aid to give her a still more valid claim against His Beloved Name.

"Mama, a Jew must give a tithe of his wealth and you have already been assessed from on high with more than a tenth. Is that fair?"

I felt I had made a strong point. I was convinced that such an argument could not be ignored.

My mother immediately saw the justice of my plea to the Master of the Universe and began to lament once more.

"Lord of the Universe, a Jew must offer up a tithe of his wealth and you have already assessed me with much more than a

140

tithe. Is that right?"

I was somewhat appeased. It pleased me that my mother, an adult, made use of exactly my words in her cause against God. I felt that we had cornered Him. I, my mother, and Herzke had won the issue. Against such an argument there could be no justificatioı. at all. God Himself must now be ashamed; but what a pity, the damage had been done! The waxen-yellow doll would never again become a living Herzke. However, the more my mother directed my words to the whitewashed ceiling, the more gratified I felt. Our side had won, and up there they were at a loss for a satisfactory reply!

Soon a Jew with a blind eye and halting gait entered. At his side he carried a chest held with a strap. He shuffled in sideways as if wanting to sneak in. He looked like a musician with an unstrung mandolin. My mother jumped up. He stood with helpless shoulders and, as man to man, sought protection from my father, who had led him into the house . . . .

I begged my neighbor's forgiveness for my long trance.

"My mother is very ill," I explained and the thought suddenly flashed through my mind: Is she still alive?

The sun-parched grass appeared to be sailing by the window. An old dog barked at the train. A small somber lad waved his cap. A thick copse seized hold of the sun and splattered it into a thousand specks of light, gilding the trees.

My companion suddenly glanced at his watch and his face lit up.

"Another half hour and you reach your goal. Exactly thirty-two minutes—why, not even thirty-two minutes!"

He grew increasingly excited at the prospect.

"Of twenty years of self-exile there remain"—his watch was in his hand—"precisely thirty-one minutes."

He peered out of the window and became cheerfully restless. He did not put away his watch but continued counting the minutes.

The more excited he became over my minutes, the more there came to life in my mind an unknown convict, with a wild mop of hair and bristling beard—part of a characteristic anecdote, episode, or maybe legend about Chekhov. And I was now experiencing that episode, I with my flushed face at the open window, and he with his watch in hand.

A convict who had been released after some ten years in Siberia was returning home to his parents, This bit of news, stuck away in a corner of a page, had made such an impression on Chekhov that he was unable to drive it from his thoughts for several days. He could not rest. He kept track of the itinerary, from city to city. He studied maps and timetables until he knew to the minute when the convict would reach home to embrace aged parents. It was a long and difficult journey, and the eventful day found Chekhov so upset in joyful anticipation that he could not control his restlessness. He kept pulling out his watch—four more hours, two more hours, one hour, a half hour . . . .minutes! Thus had Chekhov experienced that entire drama of liberation.

"Man, you have about two or three minutes more! Perhaps not even that!"

There were several long sharp blasts of the locomotive whistle. At first, factory chimneys appeared and then a number of huts surrounded by gardens. It was already near nightfall and the ramshackle but neat houses were mirroring themselves in the cooler rays of the sun.

The Polish youth was standing at my side, his hand on my shoulder as if to make easier for me that last weary minute. There were tears in his eyes. The train was coming to a stop. Simultaneously with the conductor the young Pole sang out joyously:

"Lublin!"

142